MOUNTAIN COMBAT

She bounced to her feet to circle, knife in hand, facing the warrior on the cliff. He was eyeing her warily.

She feinted, lunged, and tripped him as he reacted. Again he twisted to his feet, lithe as a cougar, and faced her, his expression unreadable beneath the stripes denoting a raid that were painted onto his skin. But a tongue of rock extended from a crag behind him, and he was backing away.

She dropped and rolled again, striking with her feet against his legs and taking them from under him. He wavered, his arms flailing for balance, the knife flying away to clatter among the stones of the cliff face. He was on the brink of the drop, the ridge ankle-high behind him.

She half rose and butted him in the stomach. . . .

THE UNTAMED

MOUNTAIN MAJESTY

Mountain Majesty

BOOK TWO

THE
UNTAMED

JOHN KILLDEER

BANTAM BOOKS

NEW YORK · TORONTO · LONDON · SYDNEY · AUCKLAND

THE UNTAMED

A Bantam Domain Book / July 1992

DOMAIN and the portrayal of a boxed "d" are trademarks of Bantam Books, a division of Bantam Doubleday Dell Publishing Group, Inc.

The Mountain Majesty series is a creation of Siegel & Siegel, Ltd.

ISBN 0-553-28886-5

Published simultaneously in the United States and Canada

Bantam Books are published by Bantam Books, a division of Bantam Doubleday Dell Publishing Group, Inc. Its trademark, consisting of the words "Bantam Books" and the portrayal of a rooster, is Registered in U.S. Patent and Trademark Office and in other countries. Marca Registrada. Bantam Books, 666 Fifth Avenue, New York, New York 10103.

PRINTED IN THE UNITED STATES OF AMERICA

RAD   0 9 8 7 6 5 4 3 2 1

TO THOSE WHO HAVE HAD
THE COURAGE TO GO INTO
A WILD AND UNTAMED LAND
AND TO SURVIVE THERE
WITHOUT TRYING TO CHANGE IT

chapter

— 1 —

Spring was greening the grasslands beyond the Belle Fourche, and buffalo, mule deer, and smaller beasts were busy on the plain and along the river, making hunting easy. Cleve liked to take his bow and stalk small game for the pot, perfecting his skills with the weapon at the same time as he provided meat.

Henri, his partner in their trapping venture, was a master hand with food, and Cleve wondered if cookery was somehow bred into the bones of Frenchmen. Back in his early days on the Missouri with the Ashworth Trapping Company, he had learned that either of the older French trappers guiding the expedition could take anything but shavings and willow bark and make something edible out of it.

Henri Lavallette could put his iron pot to simmering on the tripod over the outside fire, drop into it bits of dried leaf from his store in the shanty, along with rabbits, woodchuck, badgers, even jaybirds, and what came out was tempting and tasty. When he added roots, leaves of herbs and such, it was better still.

Even Second Son, Cleve's Cheyenne wife, had to admit that the old trapper's stew, roast meat, and bread made of pounded seeds was good. Most women would have been put out at letting a man do all the cooking, but Second Son was not a woman—not to her people and not to herself. She was a warrior and hunter of the Burning Heart Band of the Tsistsistas, skilled at war and raiding and tracking man or animal over difficult terrain; such matters as food she left to those willing to tackle them, unless she was alone on a long trail and had to prepare her own rations.

Only at night was she a woman, alone in the tipi she had shown Cleve how to set up, using the hides her people had given him and the poles she helped him cut from the hills along the river. Then she was such a woman as even the raunchy Frenchmen in Ashworth's original band, who had spun winter tales of amorous adventure and conquest, had never dreamed.

It was like making love to a panther or a she-wolf, tense and breathless, with a hint of danger. Sometimes when Cleve emerged from their tipi at dawn, he sported tooth marks and bruises. Second Son seemed proud of her own marks of affection, which she bore like the eagle feathers that dangled from her hair as symbols of her prowess.

Yet she was not like those harlots the Frenchmen

had described. Love was, to her, a thing to be enjoyed intensely in its own time, but it was not to be over-used. Her people, she told him, did not make more children than they could feed.

Cleve's dog, Snip, bounced ahead as the young trapper moved through the early light, swinging by their ears the three jackrabbits he had skewered with expertly aimed arrows. Cleve was wondering what would happen if Second Son became pregnant. Would she tame down, as white women did when with child, or would she remain the wild, free creature he knew?

A whistle shrilled through the morning. An eagle? No. By now he recognized even the most expert birdcall if it issued from human lips. This was Second Son's signal that someone had been sighted on the plain.

Cleve tucked the rabbits into his belt and set off at a run. This was dangerous country. Even now—he had reckoned it up and figured it must be 1825—relatively few Americans dared the plains. Most whites were French *coureurs de bois*, who had been coming there over the years since their homeland claimed the middle of this huge continent. A whistle meant that any sort of company might be on the horizon.

They had already encountered Piegan, and those nine dead were hidden in a mass grave beside the river downstream. Absaroka were moving, Second Son told them, as well as Kiowa, Pawnee, Lakota, and other tribes. Spring brought game and wild plants that the Indians harvested. Almost any tribe might be found here where the river watered game and the Black Hills to the south and east offered riches in lodgepoles and woodland plants.

Her own people hunted this land, though less frequently than most. The summer gathering of the entire tribe usually took place farther east, where the stretches of plain allowed huge congregations of buffalo to gather. Could the newcomers be Cheyenne?

Cleve slowed as he neared the river, slipping between the fat cottonwoods, dropping into the cover of the riverbank, and approaching the site of their camp with caution. One never knew who would be waiting.

This time it was Henri. "You hear the wheestle?" he asked, his oddly mismatched eyes, one green, one gray, busy checking out the area.

"Your woman, she never nervous, so when she signal, Henri, he get very careful, *n'est-ce pas?*"

"That makes a pair of us," Cleve said. He dropped the rabbits onto the stump where game was dressed and took out his skinning knife. With expert motions, he skinned and gutted the animals, disjointed them deftly, and dropped them into the ever-simmering pot, whose heavy lid kept the aromas from escaping to betray the position of the camp.

Then, at a nod from the Frenchman, Cleve pulled the ball from his rifle, reloaded powder, ball, and patch, and primed the pan, after checking frizzen and flint. If they were to have company, it was best to be prepared.

Together, the two moved across the river in Henri's canoe, sliding downstream under cover of the bank until they reached the level of the black stub that formed the Bad Gods' Tower. Another whistle greeted them as they sank the canoe in an eddy in a shallow creek and climbed the farther bank. This one was a warning, sure enough.

Stooping, they ran across the rough ground between the river and the volcanic core that was the mountain. The organ-pipe pillars of rock formed crevices and crannies from which an ambush was easy, and the slanting slabs of fallen stone gave access to the upper parts of the height.

Cleve ran up such a sloping course, leaving Henri to dig himself in among the debris at the foot of the truncated cone. Tucking himself into a handy nook, Cleve gave a whistle of his own, this one soft, aimed at a specific distance and not audible out on the grasslands below.

From around the curve and slightly above, he heard a twitter, a bird sound so natural that he could hardly believe it came from the lips of his wife. Then she was beside him, crouching against him in the cleft of rock, her finger pointing toward the plain lying between the tower and the distant hills.

Moving specks made dark dots against the pale green grass of spring: horses, he realized, some ridden, some riderless. A herd was being driven at top speed toward the west.

"Absaroka." Her breath was warm against his ear, and even in such circumstances Cleve felt himself becoming aroused. But he controlled that, as he was learning to control everything; the Cheyenne were not driven by their bodies but used them as tools and weapons, relying upon endurance and determination for survival. This was not a country that forgave weakness or self-indulgence, and she was teaching him that lesson.

Now, on the very edge of his vision, there came another group of riders, charging furiously after the horses and the raiders. "Pawnee," came the whisper against his ear. "Very angry."

Cleve watched the race across the plain until the

bunched horses and their pursuers were out of sight beyond the farthest swell. Then he turned to Second Son.

"When those fellows come back, they're going to be mad as hornets. We're going to have to keep close watch. It's a good thing the beaver are shedding with warm weather and we don't have to keep the traps out, but it's sure going to cut into baling the plews.

"We need to get them ready to move. Soon as the weather steadies down and there's no more chance of snow, Henri wants to head out for Lisa's Fort, up on the Yellowstone, and trade them. He's got almost as many as all our packhorses can manage, and that's dangerous, with Terrebonne's fur thieves keeping watch."

"Terrebonne." Second Son's tone was flat.

Cleve wondered yet again what had happened between her and the trapper during that earlier winter when she had rescued the Frenchman from the snow. Something drastic had taken place, he knew, but he also knew better than to ask the question outright. Second Son would tell him, if the time ever came when it was important for him to know.

"You might follow the Pawnee up the river. Not on the horse, for that might betray you to them; afoot. You run faster than I," she said, her tone at its most practical.

She was never one to consider personal pride; Cleve knew that, even so soon in their marriage. If she thought it sensible to keep watch on the Pawnee, that was the thing to do.

She knew those people as he could not. She had stolen enough horses from them, herself, to understand their reaction to that sort of raid.

"Sure enough," he said. He slid down the slanting

ramp, and his wife leaped lightly after him, landing in his arms at the foot of the slope. He gave her a quick hug.

"You and Henri can bale up the skins, and maybe I'll be back quick enough to help. But you take care, hear me? That Frenchman may be old, but he's a horny bastard. I see him watching you, sometimes."

Second Son's lips thinned into a tight smile. "I have had . . . experience . . . with Fransay before. Do not worry. I am a warrior, remember?"

And it was true. Even in the mock battle in which she had won him as her "wife," she had been a formidable opponent. He had been hard put to hold his own, and when she set her foot on his neck, it had not been because he had thrown the fight in order to win her.

He might be a lot bigger, but she knew tricks that even the *coureurs de bois* had never mentioned while instructing their young comrades of the Ashworth group about the world into which they were going. He hated to think of fighting her in earnest.

The two returned to the hidden cabin and the tipi they shared in a clump of cottonwoods beyond it. Cleve put on his stoutest pair of moccasins and added to his possibles bag powder and ball, extra frizzen and flint, all things he might need. He capped his powder horn tightly; it was a gift from Henri because he had lost his own "white man's" supplies to the Arickara almost a year before on the Missouri.

But he also took his bow and his arrows. He had found that in many circumstances it was good to have a silent weapon that did not mark your position with a cloud of black smoke. Cub, nephew of Second Son, had taught him well during his long stay with the Burning Heart Band led by her brother.

When he set out upriver, he stayed on the other side for miles, running easily, aiming to intersect the track of the horse thieves and their pursuers. The ground was rough, but by now he had run, he felt certain, over half the Great Plains, and his muscles were hardened to it.

His heart pumped steadily, and his breath came regularly and without effort. At long intervals he paused to rest and drink from the river, but he covered ground at a good rate.

He cut the track of the stolen horses just after dawn the next morning. While one unshod pony's track is much like that of any other, he was able to distinguish the hoof marks because those behind were crumbled less at the edges than those ahead.

The Pawnee were still chasing their animals, fuming with rage he was sure. If he waited downstream, holing up so as to be hidden when they came back along their route, he would know just where they were headed.

If they moved toward the tower or the river near the trapping camp, he could hightail it downstream to find one of Henri's flimsy spare canoes, which were kept at intervals up and down the Belle Fourche. That would shoot him down to his companions, at this time of year when the stream ran bank full, faster than anyone could ride.

It was a long wait, and a spring storm did not make it any more comfortable. Rain mixed with sleet scoured the grasslands and rattled like shot among the leaf buds above his hiding place. The patch of bushes he had chosen was scant cover against such weather, but the cougar-hide cloak given him by one of Second Son's fellow Cheyenne was light enough to carry on such a run. He huddled into its supple folds and waited with the patience he was learning from Second Son.

Night came and went, and near midday he felt the vibration in the ground that told him horses were coming. Bending his ear to the ground, he heard the thud of hooves and knew that the Pawnee were returning. He must find a spot from which he could watch the direction they took from the crossing.

Cleve crawled through the cold, wet bushes, icy grass touching his face and freezing his hands. There was a clump of cottonwoods that some past wind-storm had blown into a wild tangle spanning the river. Hidden at its edge, he was sure that he could see without being seen.

The butt of the easternmost tree reared from the ground, holding up a great chunk of dirt and roots like a wall. Cleve maneuvered to get behind that, in the angle of trunk and root ball. There he waited for what seemed hours, behind the fringe of feeder roots sticking out of the upper edge that provided excellent cover.

At last, during midafternoon, he heard the line of warriors splashing up out of the stream. He stared out cautiously, to see the thin line of Pawnee driving ahead of them something like half the number of horses they had lost the day before. They looked dead beat; the horses they rode were drooping, the riders not much better off. There had been a hot chase and a stiff fight, Cleve thought.

Even as he considered the bedraggled group, he heard behind him a twitter that did not come from a bird. Then something lanced through him, pinning his left arm, just below the shoulder, to the tree trunk.

He was helpless, his rifle crushed between his chest and the tree. His knife was in his belt, but it, too, was out of reach unless he could free himself. Knowing too well the swiftness with which a warrior could loose arrows, he understood that any movement would bring another shaft that might well kill him outright, caught as he was.

There was only one thing to do, and by now he had seen enough dead men to do it well. He gurgled harshly, flopped a bit, making the arm give him hell, and went limp, his eyes half-open, his eyeballs rolled back as far as he could make them go. The swaddling fur would hide from his attacker the fact that his arrow had not found his victim's heart. The blood was real enough, for certain.

If he had been forced to hang from the arrow, he couldn't have done it without betraying the fact that there was still life in him, but luckily he had "died" with his feet under him. He could take off most of the weight while still making it look as if he were dead as dirt.

His worst fear was that the warrior, whoever he was and why ever he was here instead of with the rest of his band, would take the time to scalp him. That would be nasty. But he was caught, no two ways about it, and he just had to wait and see what happened next.

There came a long cry from the plain east of the river. The sound of cautious steps rustled among dead leaves, scraped on dried bark as the scout climbed the tangle, looked down for a moment on his victim, and turned away. Twigs rustled and snapped as he descended the other side, and after some minutes Cleve heard the sound of another horse, very near, moving away into the icy grassland.

Which was all very well and good. Still he waited, however, not trusting the wily savages not to have another scout covering the river. He should have expected this one, and he cursed himself as he worked quietly at the shaft pinning him to the dead cottonwood.

That was no good at all. The head of the arrow had gone solidly into the wood, and there was no way he could get at it, even if he'd been able to reach the knife. He had to reach around behind, which was no easy task, and break off the feathered end.

He had the long Bennett arms, which turned out to be a blessing. With his right hand, he reached back, feeling demons with red-hot pincers at work inside his muscle as he moved, and snapped off the tough wood of the shaft, leaving the stub free. Then, with one desperate heave, he pushed himself backward, pulling the wood through the wound it had made.

That was not even a little bit of fun. Blood was pouring down front and back, the hot flood soaking his deerhide tunic and leggings. He would freeze, for the wind was now coming down from the northwest in gusts that found their way even into the nook protected by the uprooted trees.

This was one of those late storms that often brought snow to the plains and blizzards to the mountains. He tugged the cougar hide about him as best he could and turned blindly toward the Belle Fourche. He must move or freeze, and he began setting one foot ahead of the other, ignoring the pain in his arm.

He had to get back downriver. Already he felt light-headed from blood loss, and he had a hard time keeping his wits enough to pack torn-off bits of fur from his cougar hide into the entrance and exit holes as he moved. He knew he'd better stop that flow if he intended to get anyplace at all, and though the packing was painful, it did, in time, lessen the bleed-ing to a trickle.

He knew more or less where a canoe was hidden. Henri had drawn him a map in the dirt, showing the dead snag extending over the river, the sharp elbow of stone jagging out into the water, and the protected pool downstream from the spot where he had sunk this vessel of his flimsy navy.

If he could get there, the current would carry him down to the camp, and he knew Second Son would be watching. Not even a hawk in the sky or a badger under the ground escaped her attention.

Night was coming on fast, for the cloud cover still floated close to the ground and the wind carried more sleet along its blast. Cleve clung to tree trunks to balance himself as he staggered stubbornly forward, his feet numb, his arm afire, and his head floating mistily above, unconnected to the rest of him.

At last he fell headlong into a prickly mass of bushes, and only his upflung right arm kept him from losing an eye to the frozen twigs into which he tumbled. Lying there on his face, panting with effort and breathlessness, feeling his left arm as a mass of fiery misery, he thought longingly of death. He was too cold, too drained of blood, too disoriented to find his way back home again.

Mama would worry. Tim and Gene would search the woods for him, but Pa wouldn't even look up from his chores. He never would get home again, no matter how he tried . . . and that old bull buffalo he had seen in a vision (or had it been real? He couldn't remember) that stared at him with wicked eyes from a frosty face . . . it was lost now, in the fog.

Frozen fog. Icy twigs. Cleve gave a long sigh and

closed his eyes, feeling the beginning of warmth steal
up his legs.

Something brought him back, sharply, impera-
tively. Second Son! He would leave her, after just
finding her. He would lose that closeness that was like
nothing he had known in his life of abuse with Pa.
Second Son was calling him back, and he had to go.
Now.

He pushed downward with both hands and almost
screamed with the sudden agony in his left arm.
Rolling over, he managed to sit, then to pull himself
upward, using his right hand and a nearby sapling to
do the job.

His breath came in long groans, and he felt as if the
ground dipped and wavered under his feet, but he
lifted the right foot, set it down, pulled the left
forward, set it in front of the first. One step at a time,
with terrible concentration, Cleve forced his failing
body toward the river.

Once there, he turned downstream, more by instinct than vision, for by now it was dark. But he could
hear the water moving beside him, and when he came
to the leaning snag, it rammed directly into his belly,
bringing him up short.

Was this the spot? He stared toward the sound of
water, but he could see nothing but oily swirls of
lesser darkness where the eddies coiled. There was no
way he could find a sunken canoe in the darkness,
with his head spinning and his eyes blurred with pain.

He was on the wrong side of the river, miles from
his goal. He hadn't even Snip with him to guide him
right, for he'd left the dog tied near the tipi to keep
him from betraying his presence to the Pawnee.

He lifted a foot, set it down. Again and again and
again he did that, bumping into trees, crashing

through brush and patches of icy slush. If he had to walk back to his wife, then that was what he'd do. Or he'd die, and she would understand.

He didn't really know when he fell. Darkness filled him, mind and body, and he was almost warm again, or numb, which came to the same thing, when something cold pushed against his cheek, a hot tongue licked at his nose.

He groaned. "Donnn do'at, Snip!" he muttered. "Gotta sleep . . ."

The hard nose nudged sharply into his shoulder, and the wound in his arm came to life again, stabbing him with dull agony. Cleve opened his eyes, staring cross-eyed at the dog's nose, smelling on its moist, hot breath the carrion the animal had recently eaten.

"Good ol' Snip," he mumbled, wondering why he was so cold, lying on the ground. Had he fallen on his way to milk the Jersey? And what was his dog so upset about? Cleve had fallen many times before. Boys do that, because they don't watch where they step.

Again the dog nudged him, this time sending a jolt of agony through him. Shoulder . . . broken?

He struggled to reach, but his hand was so cold the fingers told him nothing about what they were touching. Hurt . . . arrow! Indians. He'd gone to watch the Pawnee.

Now he remembered a bit, though it was as if his head were stuffed with fog and snow. The Missouri was a long way to the northeast. Now he was a man, and Pa couldn't whip him, ever again. He had a friend. A trapper. Yes. And a wife!

Fumbling his wits together, Cleve struggled to sit and then to stand. The dog nudged close, trying to help, and before long the man found himself more or less upright, leaning against a tree that was hidden by the darkness. "Good dog," he said, though even his tongue seemed to be numb now. "Keep goin'. Sec' Son, she'll come help in a while."

Snip whined anxiously, and his tail whipped against Cleve's legs. "Arr-yow!" the dog yowled, as if urging him to walk again.

With his dog there at his side, it didn't seem quite so hard to lift those stubborn feet, to force his drained body forward. When he paused, on the edge of unconsciousness, Snip nosed him or nipped him gently on the leg to get him started again.

From time to time he was forced to halt and lean against a tree or drop flat on the ground, unable to go on. And yet every time, when the dog decided it was time to move again, Cleve dragged himself up, an inch at a time, his wounded arm and shoulder weighted with misery, and went ahead through the darkness.

The last time he fell he simply could not rise. Snip whined and whimpered, dug with his nose, nudged and worried at his master, but Cleve could only groan. At last he felt the dog lick his cheek with a wet tongue. The sound of pattering paws moved away over the frozen debris of the riverbank.

That was all right. Snip wouldn't want to see him die. Second Son didn't much care for the dog, but she would see to him just because he belonged to her man. And Henri . . . would the Frenchman help Second Son, just because she was Cleve's wife? They weren't friends yet, just partners forced together by circumstances. He wondered what would happen between those two, for he had sensed sparks of something when Lavallette looked at the warrior woman.

But his mind drifted, awash with pain, and he let go all his thoughts, trying to ease his miserable body.

Then it was peaceful, as the cold numbed him further, the blood leaked from his wounds around the tufts of fur he had stuffed into them, and morning began lightening the sky to a faintly paler gray. Cleve could think of nothing now, though he knew he was no longer in Missouri. Ma and Pa and the boys were lost in the past, along with that devil buffalo. His totem . . . he tried to laugh and couldn't.

Henri and Second Son were mere whispers at the edge of his thought. A sudden clarity gripped him and he knew that he would die here on the bank of the Belle Fourche, his ambitions unfulfilled and his dreams lost forever.

That was good. Life had been, except for these few weeks with Second Son, a painful experience for him. Death, with all its unknowns, could hardly be more terrifying.

He settled silently into a doze that would, he knew, end in the longest sleep of all.

And that was when he heard the call, shrill and clear, from downriver. A rapid beat of paws came rushing toward him, amid a flurry of hoarse barks.

Damn! He was going to live, anyway. Second Son would see to that.

chapter
— 2 —

As she worked with Henri to bale beaver Second Son kept listening for any sound that might carry above the riffle of wind and the spat of sleet or the cold gurgle of water in the creek beside the cabin. Snip, still tied, sat impatiently at the end of his tether, keeping an eye on her between bouts of chewing at the rawhide thong that held him.

She wished she had persuaded Cleve to take the dog with him, and she ignored the tattered section of the leash. If Snip escaped and went after his master, it would not have been she who loosed him. There would be some comfort in knowing that Yellow Hair had a companion, out there in the chill of the late storm.

She kept as far from Henri as possible, for it had become obvious as they worked that he had only half his mind on baling the plews. His strange eyes seemed to be fixing their gray-green gaze on her more often than on the thongs he bound around the bundles of furs.

In her role as a warrior, Second Son had not lived for nineteen summers without learning much about the ways of men, and she knew what was in his mind. While her people were rigidly controlled among their own kind, rape was something that was acceptable with women of other tribes.

The day crept by, and as night fell she could almost hear the thoughts of the Frenchman as he watched her go to her tipi and slip inside. He was thinking of following, she knew, and that would mean killing him. Yellow Hair said they needed him as a partner, so she wanted to avoid that if possible.

Second Son made it a point to come out again and sit in the shelter of the tipi, her metal knife, for which she had traded long ago with this very man, on her knee. She ran the sharpening stone up and down the steel, making a soft singing sound of metal on stone, as the sleet fell on the tipi and pattered among the bushes and in the treetops.

Henri did not come near her home, and for that she was grateful. It was enough that she was worried about Yellow Hair.

That puzzled her. Never before had she worried about a warrior who was doing a necessary task, no matter what its risks. She had not worried about herself as she raided or hunted or made her solitary monthly rides over the plains or into the hills. A warrior did what was necessary, and if he died, that was a part of living and nothing terrible.

But now it was as if some thong stretched between her body and that of the man she had won in fair combat. The closeness they shared was unlike what she felt for her brother and his family or even her father and aunt. It was as if a part of her had followed him up the Belle Fourche, leaving her diminished.

She shook away the sleet on the fur about her shoulders, put away her knife, and rose. There was nothing she could do in the darkness, although she felt strongly that her husband had need of her help.

By first light, however, she would be on her way upstream. She knew that Snip would be ahead of her, for the thong was almost severed when she tied him for the night, just inside her shelter.

The wind cried above the river and rattled tree branches. Lying alone where she had only lain with Cleve, Second Son listened until she forced herself to close her eyes and sleep. It would not help either of them if she were too weary tomorrow to be alert and strong.

She was up when the wind died away in the last dark hours before dawn. Before the cutting blast started in again, she wrapped herself warmly in her robe, armed herself with bow and knife, and set out upriver on the eastern side, having crossed the stream in Henri's home camp canoe.

Snip was, as she had known he would be, far ahead. It was the sound of his feet crunching in the sleet before the tipi that had wakened her in the silent hours.

When light seeped thinly across the grasslands, she paused in a thick clump of willow to stare over the wide reaches; there was no motion of men on horse-back topping the swells. The Pawnee had either returned already to their hunting camp in the hills, or they had not come at all. Where was Yellow Hair?

But she did not intend to lose time in wondering. She kept the murmur of the water on her right, the lighter sky now covering the grasslands on her left, and moved lightly and swiftly up the Belle Fourche, keeping her ears sharp for any sound outside the normal ones of a chilly spring morning.

When Snip's excited barking rang through the cold morning, she raised her head and shouted in return, the high call she used with her own family. She listened for some reply from Cleve, but only the river and the sleet could be heard.

It was a long time before she saw the dog bouncing through the trees, his tail upright, his ears cocked, every part of his body speaking to her as well as if he possessed words like a man. He had found his master, and he was coming after her.

She ran, ignoring the possibility of lingering Paw-nee or spies for rival trappers. When she came at last to the sodden shape that was her husband, she went onto her knees and felt him over with anxious fin-gers. Except for the arrow wound, which was packed with fur from his cougar hide, he was uninjured, but she could see by the blue tint of his skin that he had lost a great deal of blood and was chilled deeply.

That was something her people knew about, as was the best way of moving an unconscious person who was far too heavy to carry. Second Son went with her knife among the willows at the side of the stream and cut long poles, binding three at a bunch together with thongs from her pouch.

Those were strong enough to bear the weight they

must hold, she knew. She dragged those to Cleve's side and laid them along his length, measuring the space she needed. She split her robe of heavy doubled deerhide, and after moving the poles side by side, she wrapped them in the width of the leather and laced it together again with more thongs. Then she called to Snip, who came close, sniffing curiously at the contraption.

Rolling Cleve onto the makeshift travois, Second Son bound him in place with his own cougar robe, tying the folds tightly about him to keep what little warmth he might still possess inside his body. Then she tied Snip between the forward poles and caught the foremost thongs in her right hand.

Cheyenne dogs knew all about dragging travois, but she was far from certain that this white man's animal would understand what she wanted. But Snip, after sitting down and staring up at her with puzzled eyes, seemed to catch the idea as soon as she began to pull. He rose and set his weight into the thong harness, and together they moved the unconscious man down the river toward shelter, food, and the fire that Henri would have built as soon as he rose.

It was slow going, and she had to change hands, for the stooping position required to reach the thongs was wearying on the back. Second Son stopped only when Snip sat, his tongue lolling, his sides heaving with his heavy panting. Once the dog was able to pull again, they were off, and before noon they were drawing near the spot where Second Son had hidden the canoe.

From the farther bank she whistled her signal to the Frenchman. She needed help to get Cleve into the canoe without damaging the frail craft, and she was not a good canoeist at best. Her people had no need to travel on water, and that was not a skill they knew.

She pushed the canoe into the water and paddled across to meet the bulky shape of Henri, who lumbered down the bank and stepped expertly into the vessel with agility strange in one so huge.

"I have found him, and the dog and I have dragged him there." She pointed to the spot where Snip sat, tail thumping the ground from time to time as he eyed his master, who was only a featureless lump along the ground.

The wind had lessened, the sleet of the day before reduced to only an occasional flurry, so it was easier to reach the farther bank and secure the canoe. Henri lifted Cleve as if he were a child and laid him in the bottom of the craft. Second Son found herself, not for the first time, envying the size that gave a man the advantage over even the strongest of short women. The leverage, the height; those were important, too.

"He is bad, these Cleve," murmured the trapper, his arms propelling the canoe swiftly through the gray swirls of the river and up the swifter ones of the creek. "I see that *couleur* before, *n'est-ce pas*? Is bad business, that."

In the mixture of Cheyenne, English, and French that the trio had devised for communication, Second Son said, "I have seen worse, among my people. We know how to treat such things. I have herbs in my packs, and I have watched the Wise Woman at her work. I will save him, Fransay!"

Something about her tone made the Frenchman chuckle wryly. "Perhaps you will, warrior woman. It would not surprise me, for you are a mos' astonishing *femme*. Yet do not despair, should he die. Old Henri will offer you—" But her piercing glance upward from Yellow Hair's face stopped the words in his throat.

The prow of the craft nudged against the soft bank of the creek at last, and she leaped out and dragged it up the slant until it was steady. Henri stepped out and bent over his partner, lifting him easily.

"Into the tipi," said Second Son. "I will make a fire."

"Now that is not good," the Frenchman protested. "It will take the time, and he is chill to the bone. *Chez moi*, there is already fire, a pot of stew is cook there, and there is room to work. Come there, *ma petite*. That is the best plan, eh?"

She thought swiftly. Though she hated to admit it, he was right. To take the time to build a fire and more time for it to warm the tipi might put Yellow Hair at risk for the coughing sickness. It was best to go where it was already warm, where food waited.

She nodded agreement and followed him into the shanty hidden among the cottonwoods and willows. The single room was smoky, but it smelled deliciously of stew.

Henri put Cleve down on his own bed, which was made of layered skins of all kinds and topped with a luxurious covering of dressed beaver furs, laced together to form a sort of quilt. Second Son pulled this away so that as the wound was treated and bled afresh it would not be spoiled.

Then she knelt on one side of the pallet, facing Henri on the other, and the two of them began peeling away the blood-stiffened leather from Cleve's shivering body. Rising, she hung the beaver quilt over the back of Henri's rude chair so that it would warm before the fire. Then she returned to stripping her man and cleaning the blood and muck from his skin.

Picking out the fluff he had thrust into the entry

and exit wounds was a nasty job, which the woman's nimble fingers managed with finesse. As she took the last strands of fur from the puckered holes, Henri brought out the fine knife he kept for surgery.

"I clean this," he said. "I am ver' good at that, for many wound have I fix in my life."

Second Son nodded and withdrew her fingers as the Frenchman sliced away the dark flesh from the wound, poking into the oozing hole to remove the remnants of dirt and leather and fur. Then they turned the wounded man and Henri cleansed the other side of his upper arm, taking out all foreign matter and cutting a clean slit, after he drenched the skin with the whiskey he had saved from his last trip out to the trading fort.

They bound the cuts tightly together, wrapping the arm with soft leather and then binding it to his chest with more. Cleve's teeth were chattering now, and fever was rising in him, as she could tell by the fiery feel of his body. As soon as they rolled him, head to heels, in the hot fur wrappings, she turned to the Frenchman.

"I go to find willow bark," she said. "You have water boiling in that pot?" She pointed to the heavy can Henri used to boil his coffee.

"I will empty it and set clean water to heat," he assured her. "You make the tea to break the fever, *oui?*"

She did not answer but swept through his blanket door and out into the late afternoon. The wind was rising again, this time carrying a burden of the wet, heavy snow of spring.

Though it was still far from sunset, the sky was dark and shadows were thick beneath the cotton-woods. It would be night in less than an hour. She followed the creek to its mouth and there she plunged down the riverbank into a tangle of willows, which already showed buds. She pulled down a young tree and stripped off a number of limber branches, which she bundled and tied across her back.

As Second Son moved up the slope again, toward the higher ground along the creek bank, she paused and lifted her head, listening. Above the growing whine of the wind, she could hear another whistle, shrill and compelling. It came from the direction of the tower beside the river, but the cloud was so low and black that it was impossible even to see the thick stub of rock beyond the dim line of trees.

She hitched her burden around so that the willow would not catch on the growth that lined the banks. Then she moved upstream along the creek, halfway down in the shelter of the bank. That might be Terrebonne again, or one of his lookouts. It certainly was not any tribe she knew, for those would communicate with birdcalls or the long howls of the wolf.

Whatever whistled on the Bad Gods' Tower, she had no intention of betraying her presence to it as she made her way with some difficulty along the damp creek bank toward Henri's cabin. When she emerged at last in the hidden nook where it sat, she gazed for a long time at the dark bulk of the building. No chink of fire showed outside, and for that she was grateful, for whoever was on that mountain was more likely an enemy than a friend.

chapter
— 3 —

When the comforting numbness wore off, Cleve woke and cursed. He had been vaguely aware when Second Son moved him and Henri lifted him into the canoe, but he was so nearly frozen that he felt nothing but a minor twinge, even when his leg flopped over awkwardly and his ankle cracked against the side of the craft.

When they went to work on his arrow wound, he fainted for the first time in his life, and he was grateful for it. The blackness that welled up behind his eyes was welcome, and when it receded, he tried his best to hold it about him like a blanket, keeping the pain from becoming altogether real. The bitter dose Second Son held to his lips, however, brought him to consciousness.

Cleve shook all over, his teeth rattling against the tin cup, which was very hot. The liquid was hot as well, and he almost strangled on the first sip, but Henri's arm went under his shoulders to lift him and a hand smacked his back, sending waves of pain outward from his wound. He drank again, getting the medicine down without choking, and the two let him lie back and rest.

"Snip . . ." he murmured as Second Son wiped his forehead with a handful of moss. "He came."

Her dark eyes smiled down at him. "A dog that is a friend, I think, is something worth having. I would have found you in time, Yellow Hair, but he made it happen faster. And now you need to rest, sleep; do not dream."

He obeyed gladly, shivering still, but finding the willow-bark tea taking effect, warming him and breaking the fever that gripped him. He drifted off, feeling sweat on his temples and in his hair. The deep shuddering that had shaken him to the core was almost gone.

The last thing he saw was Second Son's silhouette, erect and alert against Henri's fire, keeping watch over him. Snip lay at her feet, but Henri was only a burring snore in the darkness beyond the glowing coals. The quiet scene was soothing, and his eyes closed as sleep took him.

When he woke, Cleve felt as if he had been drained of all, instead of a goodly portion, of his blood. His legs wavered like young reeds as Second Son helped him out to relieve himself; his vision tended to blur. Fever racked him again, and his hands shook, so that it was hard to help Second Son hold the cup to his lips.

This time it held strong broth from Henri's stew, and the juices of meats and roots and young shoots went straight into his blood. When he had drunk all he could, he lay back again and sighed. "Did the Pawnee come?" he asked his wife, his voice sounding as if it rose from the bottom of a well.

He'd never been so weak since he was a little boy and had scarlet fever and Mama sat up with him for many nights, nursing him through. This was not a condition that he liked, but there was nothing to be done about it. Cleve knew he had to keep eating and sleeping and hoping that mortification didn't set in, deep inside his arm.

"I heard a whistle last night when I went after bark," she said. "Not Pawnee nor any of my kind. We do not whistle in that way, but with the calls of hawks or eagles. I think someone watches again, up there on the tower. Henri has gone to look, but he should return soon."

Cleve closed his eyes, feeling the room spin slowly about him as the combination of bark tea and broth took effect. He felt as if a breeze could pick him up and carry him away as effortlessly as it spun an autumn leaf from a tree.

He had to concentrate on getting stronger. This was probably the last of the spring storms, and before long the Frenchman would be ready to go out with his bales of fur to trade at the fort up on the Yellowstone.

Cleve drifted into and out of sleep for what seemed a very long time. The sound of movement inside the room, along with Henri's voice, woke him at last to see the trapper leaning over the fire, warming his hands. There was a rank smell in the air, even worse than the normal stench of the Frenchman and his living quarters.

". . . little *bâtard*, he watch us, *oui*? That Terrebonne, he send another of his spy. I do not know these Pierrot, but he watch no more, *n'est-ce pas*?"

Cleve strained to see what Henri held up in the firelight. A dollar-sized bit of scalp holding a hank of long hair. Not the black of Indian hair, it was brown, with glints of red that caught the light of the flames. Another of Terrebonne's lookouts?

"More spies, Henri?" he managed to ask in a tone that was weaker than he liked.

"It seem so. Make me ver' angry, you know. But we do not have to worry, *mon ami*, for the moment. These one is dead, and he say, before he die, that Terrebonne he have go back into the Beeghorns to his main camp.

"He send small Pierre to see where we go from here. He know about my great trap ground beyond the mountains, and he want to know just where that might be." Henri's laugh was grim.

"He will find that when the moon she turn purple! When fall come, we all go to my camp in the west, but until then nobody but Henri know where my beaver stream run."

Cleve spent the next days in a strange state between sleep and semiconsciousness. He knew that there was infection in the wound, for Second Son and Henri held him down and reamed it out with a ramrod heated in the fire until it glowed red as that wicked buffalo's eyes.

He thought, for a time, that he had died, and this torment was a part of the punishment his father had believed in so strongly, but his wife's continual presence reassured him about that. Nothing could be hell if Second Son was there.

From time to time he half woke, sipped at broth or medicine or water, and plunged back into a red haze of dream that held terrors he never remembered when he emerged from sleep. Hands tended him. Once Henri lifted him while his bedding was changed, and the pain of his cauterized arrow wound made him faint again.

But a day came when he opened his eyes and knew where he was and what had happened to him. He lifted a hand, but he was too weak even to hold it up and it dropped limply back onto the fur on which he lay.

Snip came to nose his cheek, and Cleve realized that Second Son and Henri must be outside, busy with the daily tasks of survival. He held on to the dog's neck and tried to sit, but it was impossible. He was too weak to lift his head, much less his upper body, so he dropped back and stared up into the smoky reaches of the roof. Soon someone would come, and then he would be able to talk sensibly again.

The woman came first, her arms filled with wood, which she put into the fire Indian fashion, ends first, so the rest could be pushed up as the other parts burned away. She busied herself at the fire for a moment. Then she turned to him.

He grinned at her, feeling the growth of hair on his cheeks bristle. He had never had much beard, and that told him how long he had been out of action.

She gasped and went to her knees, putting a hand on either shoulder, staring into his eyes. "You are yourself again, Yellow Hair!"

He managed to move a hand enough to pat her arm. "Safe and sound. Too tough to die." Just speaking exhausted him, and he contented himself with feeling her touch and seeing the expression on her usually impassive face.

There came a step at the door, and the Frenchman's bulk filled the gap, darkening the room momentarily. "So, you live, do you?" he asked, and there was something in his tone that was not entirely joyful. "Then I would do well to take *mon plaisir* while yet there is time, *n'est-ce pas?*"

Before Cleve unraveled his meaning, the trapper was upon Second Son, catching her off guard, kneeling, at his mercy. But one never caught a Cheyenne warrior entirely unaware, for those trained ears caught sounds and whispers of motion that others would never detect.

She twisted like a cat in his grasp, her body drawing into a bunch of muscle and sinew. When she unwound, her feet lashing out into his belly, her elbows striking outward, her head pounding forward into his face, even the huge Frenchman could not hold her.

She sprang free, whirling to face him, her knife appearing as if by magic in her hand. But she was hampered by the confined space, the clutter of bedding and cookpots and weapons that lay about the floor.

Cleve strained to move, to reach for his rifle, leaned conveniently near the head of his pallet, but he literally could not. Snip, worried and puzzled by the wordless struggle going on, shrank back into the space between Cleve and the wall and whined softly, uncertain whether to do anything about this strange behavior among his people.

Second Son knew better than to come within reach of those long arms, which could break her in half if they got a chance. Cleve could see her thinking as she sidled along the wall, feinting with the knife, trying to draw Lavallette out so she could slash him with its edge or stab him with its point.

But the Frenchman, too, was a seasoned fighter and he outweighed her by three times. He also knew the dangers of facing an opponent armed with a knife, and he avoided her efforts deftly. When she stepped back and her heel rolled on a billet of wood, he was ready and pounced with all his bulk.

Cleve was sweating with effort, but still he could not move. Then he knew. "Snip!" he said. "Kill him!"

Back at the fort on the Missouri, the dog had tackled a bear. Snip could give Second Son a chance, if he would understand.

The dog whined anxiously, his gaze fixed on the heaving tumble on the floor. "Snip! *Kill him.*" Cleve's voice was barely audible, but now the dog had the idea.

Snip bounced over his recumbent master and dived onto Henri's back, grabbing the nape of his neck in his jaws and worrying it like a rabbit. Growling deep in his throat, the dog loosed the Frenchman and took another hold, deeper.

With a roar of rage, Lavallette heaved upright, the animal dangling from his neck like some strange ornament, and reached back to crush his attacker. Second Son, breathless but alert, sprang up as soon as her weight was lifted. She scrambled on the floor for her knife, finding it kicked near the door.

She dived after it, spun, and went into the struggle again, this time with her blade foremost. There came an agonized gasp, a groan of *"Merde!"*

Cleve smelled blood and shit, and the big man fell forward, Second Son stepping aside just in time to keep from being felled again beneath his bulk. Snip held on for a moment, shaking the hairy neck, but once he knew the man was dead, he let go of him and returned to his master's side.

Second Son was gasping with effort as she bent over Cleve. "You are well?" she asked.

He laughed hysterically. "I should ask you that," he managed to say at last. "Is he dead?"

"I gutted him," she said. "And now we must go to our own tipi, for I will burn down this white man's house. He is too big to raise onto a burial platform. I do not care if he finds the Other Place as a man or a homeless spirit, without horses or weapons."

Cleve tried again to push himself up, but his arms were like tallow. "Sorry, little one. I can't move myself at all."

She smiled through smears of blood and the grit from the dirt floor. "I have moved you before, Yellow Hair," she said. "But first I save what we need from this Fransay's house."

Cleve was shocked. Robbing the dead was something he had been taught was unforgivable. Second Son, he had to recall very quickly, came from a very different people and was taught another way. Here there was no extra, no elbow room for wasting the property of an enemy, though the things sent into the afterworld with friends or relatives were never begrudged. He had seen fine weapons and furs and pots provided to those who died while he stayed with the Burning Heart Cheyenne.

He closed his eyes while she bustled about, gathering the extra ax, knives, and rifles, the pots and tools and traps the Frenchman had gathered over his years of using this cabin as his plains headquarters. Mama would call this thievery of the worst kind. Pa would nod and say it was just what he'd expect of any man who'd marry an Indian.

But the more he thought, the more he understood that out here in the wild country it was survival that mattered. He needed traps, and Henri had a great store of them here. They would burn what possessions they didn't take, and certainly none of them would be of use to Henri Lavallette ever again.

When he looked at the room at last, the fire burned brightly, illuminating the blackened interior, the light dancing on the oddly flattened form of the Frenchman. But much of the smaller stuff—the bags of black powder, the pouches of flints and extra frizzens and lead shot—was gone.

The bales of furs were in their own hidden shelter, concealed in a thicket under a thatch of grass and leather, and only the traps, hanging on pegs on the outside walls of the shanty, were left. Cleve could hear Second Son taking them down, the clank of metal distinct in the quiet of the evening.

It was time for him to move. If Cousin John could run for days with a bullet in his leg, as Cleve had heard him recount, surely he could get his own wavering bones out of bed and stand. The fury of seeing his wife attacked hadn't been able to push him up, and he was ashamed of that. Was he a weakling? He'd only lost half his blood and almost frozen. That shouldn't have stopped him.

Gritting his teeth, he rolled over onto his face, put his hands beneath him, and shoved hard. On the third try he made it up far enough to sit back on his heels.

Snip, who had been lying at his feet, was quivering with excitement, nosing his side, licking his elbow, trying his best to help. With an effort he hadn't known was in him, Cleve managed to crawl off the pallet of furs to the table, three strides distant, whose leg offered him a hold as he hauled himself up, hand over hand. When

Second Son reentered the cabin, he was leaning against the wall, his legs trembling beneath his weight.

"You can walk?" she asked, completely unsurprised. Her people did the impossible every day, without comment.

"I'll walk whether I can or not," he said. But it wasn't quite that easy. He leaned heavily on Second Son's shoulder as they went, and he blessed the fact that this day was really springlike, a warm breeze rippling the grasses beyond the trees, the leaves showing green tufts bursting from their tight buds. He realized he had been unconscious for a long time.

The tipi was warm, coals glowing in the firepit, his bedroll ready for him as he dropped heavily and gasped with the effort he had made. Staring up at Second Son, he said, "I think I'll live now, little warrior. If I could get from there to here, and if you'll keep me full of hot meat, I'll be up from here in no time."

"There is meat over the fire," she said. Her gaze followed Snip, who bounced out of the tipi through the door hole. "I have tasks to do."

Cleve reached with a clean stick and spun the haunch of venison that Second Son had suspended over the firepit. Its juices were beginning to sputter into the coals below it, and the smell was inviting, though the meat was far from done.

Think of the meat, Cleve told himself, trying his best not to think of what his wife was doing there in the shanty Henri had built with his great hands. In its shelter he had plotted with the Frenchman to protect them both from Terrebonne's spy and from the Blackfoot. They had, for a short while, shared a pleasant camaraderie, but Cleve found himself admitting that from the moment Second Son arrived he had known that Henri had his eye on her.

He spun the meat again, letting the crackle of juice on the fire drown out the growing crackle from outside. The shanty was blazing, he knew, for he could hear the old wood, raised there by the trapper many years before, beginning to snap like small gunshots as damp spots turned to steam and insects that had burrowed into it exploded from their own juices.

Then the flames roared upward, so intensely that he could almost see them through the buffalo-hide wall of his hidden tipi. He felt suddenly sick. Old Henri, Emile's friend, was burning with his house. What a pity, he thought. . . . He sank back onto his bedroll and lay flat in the grateful warmth and the smell of cooking food.

But now they were supplied with everything they needed in order to proceed on their own, trapping as partners and family. He no longer needed to think of catching up with Ashworth and his group, who must have gone on up the Missouri months ago or cut across country to find that rich beaver ground for which they had been headed.

If only he knew where Henri's secret trapping country was . . . Cleve's head reeled, and he pressed it back into the furs of his bed and closed his eyes. If he could bring himself to steal the man's traps, he could also steal his beaver streams.

But that was a secret lost with the Frenchman, locked in the head that was now wreathed in flames, the very skull cracking in the blaze that had been his house. Sick with the thought, Cleve turned on his side and covered his face with his hands.

Even then he seemed to see red eyes, curved horns. Through a frosty mist, the devil buffalo that had haunted his dreams since a long-ago morning on the Missouri was gazing at him with wicked understanding.

chapter
— 4 —

Defeat was a thing that Jules Terrebonne had never endured in all his life. Now, twice within too short a time, he had been defeated, and once by a woman. That bitch of the Cheyenne who called herself a warrior had castrated him as neatly and passionlessly as if he had been a bull calf, leaving him impotent and raging. Every time he pissed he thought of her with fury bordering on insanity, although a year and more had passed since he left the village of the Burning Heart.

Once again he was frustrated and furious: the fugitive that he, in company with his Piegan friends, had pursued had managed to dispose of nine seasoned Blackfoot warriors. The plan had seemed foolproof, when he and Standing Bear put it together. They had chased that unknown man who wounded Eagle Beak to the river, where he should have gone to ground, as anyone sane would do. Those who followed should have been able to root him out at their leisure.

Instead, he had joined forces with the mad trapper who set his traps along the Belle Fourche. That was a thing Terrebonne had not expected, for Henri Lavallette had always been remote, cold, and suspicious in his dealings with other white men. Even a fellow *Français* had fallen under suspicion, as Terrebonne had found for himself.

Jules and Standing Bear had agreed that Terrebonne would remain behind in the trees along the river until the main encounter with their prey was well under way. Then he would ride in, his flintlock primed, to demoralize the quarry after the Piegan had softened him up. But that one had not been alone, as they expected him to be.

However, Jules had seen his allies killed, down to the last man who had been dragged, wounded, from hiding and dispatched with a knife. He saw this with his own eyes as he moved along in the cover of the trees along the river, scouting the area beside the mountain the Sioux called the Bad Gods' Tower.

His anger had been so great that the Frenchman had almost ridden pell-mell into lone battle with those two, but he had stopped to consider. That had been his salvation, for as he plotted he saw a savage figure watching silently from the top of the black stub of stone that formed the dark mountain.

It was not one of the Piegan. It was not a white man of any breed. But it saw him, and it warned him off with an unmistakable gesture that filled his heart with a sudden chill.

He had fled, and even now he could not say exactly why, for never in all his life had Jules Terrebonne run from anyone. Was it the loss of his balls that caused this sudden cowardice? The thought filled him with even greater darkness as he rested in a thicket of young lodgepole pines, thinking of his misfortunes of the past two years.

He should have been safe from any interference from the top of that rock. Indeed, he should have been able to count upon having an ally there, for his spy, Jacques, had been set there as soon as the worst of the winter broke, in order to watch Henri Lavallette at his trapping.

When the old fool had bales and bales of fine plews ready to go out to trade, Terrebonne had planned to sweep down upon him and take them all, leaving him to retreat, grumbling, into the isolation he seemed to love so well. Henri would be like a crop, ready to harvest every two or three years if one handled him carefully, leaving him his horses and weapons and traps so that he could return to work and trap more fine furs for Terrebonne and his white and Indian henchmen to steal again and trade for good weapons and blankets, wenches and liquor. But the entry of this newcomer into the picture had changed things for the worse.

Back there in the Black Hills the greatest war chief of his Piegan allies had fallen to that unknown warrior. Eagle Beak was a hunter without equal, leader of the Bear Clan of the Piegan Blackfoot. He had surprised that stranger asleep, but it had not helped him to defeat him.

Even now, Jules could see the blood on the Piegan's

neck, the glazed eyes of the desperately wounded man. Examining the ground, later, he had traced the places where each combatant had lain, and he still marveled that anyone could shoot blind with a bow and hit his mark.

As Eagle Beak hovered between life and the Other Place, his people buzzed like disturbed bees, furious at this intruder. It had seemed a sound way to consolidate his influence with the tribe: Terrebonne would accompany Eagle Beak's kin on the trail of vengeance.

Now he regretted that decision. If he returned alone, leaving all those dead behind him, their bodies lost and their spirits unattended into the spirit world, he would not be welcomed back by the Bear Clan. He might, indeed, find himself entertained painfully by the women grieving for their lost menfolk, and that was a thought that did not please him.

No, he would go back to the Bighorns, to the main trapping camp he kept there, and gather together some of the men he had left to harvest the streams along that valley through the winter. He should be able to take a good half dozen out without disrupting the business of taking and treating plews. That would give him enough of an edge, now that he knew what to expect, to overcome those two madmen down on the Belle Fourche, who would be feeling very cocky after their destruction of the Piegans.

Let them have a month or two to settle down and begin feeling secure. He would send a scout to follow them if they left their camp. Then he would strike.

As he set off again, making a wide circle around the tower that stood, black and watchful, over the plain, he thought of the warrior he had seen standing on the dark rock, waving his weapon threateningly on the height. There had been something strangely familiar about him. But no Indian remained in place for long, and by the time Terrebonne returned with many men, it would make no difference, anyway. With enough men at his back, Terrebonne feared no one.

The grasslands, now only lightly marked with snow from the latest spring storm, rolled away ahead of the horse. Terrebonne, sunk heavily in the saddle, rode the beast at a steady pace for longer than was really good for the animal. When he stopped, he was far to the west of the tower; once out of sight, he camped, though he did not dare to risk a fire.

While those two white men would not follow, the Piegan might well decide to search for their kindred. And they would find his tracks, careful though he had been to cross rocky patches.

They could catch up to him, if they wanted, and he disliked the thought of talking his way out of his present dilemma. He had run, leaving behind his fallen brothers, and that was the fact. No Piegan would accept that when their own had been left dead beside the Belle Fourche.

In two days of hard riding, he topped a swell and saw before him the shining tops of the Bighorns glittering against the sky, which now was a clean spring blue. Above the tallest peak was a circular cloud like a lens, and he knew that somewhere high in the range it was raining.

Too bad . . . he had become lank and chilled, lacking campfires and cooked food. But soon he would begin to move among those steeps, following the stream he knew so well, climbing until he was among the forests that cloaked the middle reaches of the mountains.

He kicked his horse into a faster walk and rode down the irregular swells toward the line of trees marking a stream running down from the heights, which cut away northward to join the Powder River. He would follow it, taking its easy course into the soaring reaches of the Bighorns, as he had done so often before.

Although the foothills seemed very near in the clear air of spring, it took a day and a half of steady riding for Terrebonne to reach the first slopes. But there was water aplenty there, as the creek tumbled down from the heights, fat with snow water. Woodchucks and deer were moving about, lively with spring energy. Grizzlies were awake, too, he found as his horse climbed among the lodgepoles and he looked up at scarred patches slashed into the tree trunks by the claws of giants of the breed.

As he moved upward the way became steeper, and he was forced to lead his mount as they scrambled from rocky patch to soil pocket and back again. The air cooled even more than the chill of spring would warrant, and he drew in a deep lungful of the brisk, pine-tanged fragrance.

Night found him high on the shoulder of a mountain, heading for a saddle that would allow him to drop down into the long valley where his trappers worked. Elk bugled in the distance, but he had no need to hunt, so near his goal.

He found a rocky spot clear of bear grass and built a small fire, sheltered under the edge of a ridge of outcropping boulders. There he roasted a grouse he had potted as he rode through the forest, congratulating himself on the continuing excellence of his eye. The hot meat was sheer joy to his empty belly.

Now he began to relax, to feel that perhaps he had

not lost command of his own affairs and those of other men, as he had feared when he ran from the Bad Gods' Tower. Here he knew his way about as few ever learned, except for the Indians. Here he felt that God Himself could not gainsay the will of Jules Terrebonne.

He warmed himself thoroughly, made his bed of blankets and a buffalo robe, and lay back, staring at the starry sky, from which the clouds had been swept by a strong wind that did not reach down into his sheltered camp, though the few trees on the heights above whipped against the sky, dark against dark.

Even as he watched, there came a streak of fire across the firmament, blazing in a long arc from northeast to southwest. Jules shivered. He did not like such things, which were beyond his understanding and his control.

Was that the mark of *le bon Dieu* or of *le diable*? Or was it some causeless act of nature that no one could possibly decipher, no matter how he tried? Was it a warning, an omen?

Disturbed and discomfited, he turned on his side and poked ashes over his fire. He would sleep, and he would not dream. So he commanded himself, and once he became still, so it was.

Dawn found him up, his mount again packed with gear. Tomorrow he would come down from the high places, with the snowy peaks staring over his shoulder, and surprise his men at their work. Already mosquitos were out, hatched by the warming days, and they attacked his neck and ears, his hands and nose, while he readied himself to move. But Terrebonne knew a trick or two, and rancid tallow put off even those voracious insects, once he rubbed it into his swarthy skin, which already wore a layer of ingrained grime.

The horse was snorting and shivering its hide as the insects dug in wherever they could find a spot, but when the two began to move again, they were relieved of the worst of the creatures. Once among the pines, they climbed hard, making for the low-slung back of the ridge above them.

At midday Terrebonne stood on a spine of rock and looked down into a steep, gloomy glen. From that height it seemed nothing but trees, shoulder to shoulder in a seemingly impenetrable mass. That was the thing that made this trapping camp so secure.

The glen seemed completely unpromising, and no one in his wits would waste the time to get down there among those forbidding trees. Yet once past that first rank, growing high on the slopes on either side of the creek, he had found a valley that opened out and continued for several miles, watered by a complex of springs and creeks teeming with beaver and marmot, grouse and ptarmigan, and every sort of animal the mountains bred.

He dismounted and moved along the ridge, watching closely for the outcrop of blue stone that was the marker for his hidden path. The horse followed him without being led, as he had trained him to do, for this track was one that needed both hands, or an unwary walker might find himself impaled upon the top of a pine or alder some hundreds of feet below.

The mulchy cushion of needles and bark and deadfall had washed away with the spring runoff, to reveal the stone beneath, and Jules set his feet carefully, keeping his mind on his business. The first time he had descended this steep he slipped, and only the saints had saved him from death. A young alder, drooping still from the snows of winter, had rushed at him as he tumbled, and he grabbed at its springy bole as he moved. His shoulders still ached at the remembered strain, but it had been enough.

He had cut that alder, later, hating to owe anything, even to a tree.

The thick scent of the pines clogged his nose as he went down, and he sneezed irritably. Then he stopped, his left hand braced against a tree, as a sound echoed up the glen. A shot? Maybe one of the men was hunting, but any shot, coming unexpectedly, brought the wary Frenchman to alertness. He would go even more carefully.

Behind him, the horse pricked its ears and gave a soft whinny. That was another indication that something down there was not as it should be.

Terrebonne picked his steps carefully, though he felt a driving need to reach the overhang that would give him a view of the length of the valley. "I wish I know what happen, down there," he muttered.

As if in reply, there came a volley of shots, the deep-throated roar of muskets and the sharper note of flintlocks. The trapper took his Hawken from its thong on his saddle and cradled it in his left arm as he continued downward. That made traversing this stretch more dangerous, but it made him feel far more secure.

The ledge, when he reached it, was shadowed by the western ridges, making him invisible from the land below. He lay flat, anyway, peering over the edge, his face brushed by the tender fronds of flower stalks and new grass.

His keen eyes, trained to pick out anything unusual, caught a hint of motion downstream, near the spinney of young alders where he often hid while waiting for elk to come down to drink. Two more shapes flitted out of the spinney, moving toward the creek bank, where thick willows and birches offered good cover. They were heading down toward the stout log house his men had built for storage and shelter when trapping here.

If these were just now moving in, it meant that others already had at least some of his confreres pinned down farther along the creek, probably at the cabin itself. Terrebonne glanced up and down the valley, searching for any mounted party, but he could spy no horses. They must have left them up in the trees on the only slope gradual enough to give them secure footing.

That meant that someone finding his way secretly to the horses could stampede them downward, to the distraction of their owners and the disruption of the small battle going on in his valley.

Whatever had sent him fleeing from the Bad Gods' Tower, Terrebonne knew he was no coward. He would find a way to frighten those horses, though it meant leaving his own mount behind, tethered to a knob of rock hidden from view from above or below.

The pockets of earth clinging to the steep cliffs around which he clambered were soft with snow water, while the sheer stone pitches were slick with wet. It was a nasty business, Terrebonne decided before he got halfway to his goal. But once past the worst, he found footing along weathered ledges. Making his way required so much concentration, though, that he forgot to listen when occasional shots were fired below in the valley.

It was dark before he was off the steep, and that

made his task even more dangerous. Yet he reached
the slope, which was overgrown thickly with young
lodgepole timber after some past forest fire, and
found himself standing on soil again.

As he held himself still, listening with all his attention, he heard a soft snort. A horse, *sans doute*. He had
reached his goal.

He turned his ear toward the valley, but the firing
had stopped. Darkness and silence alone filled that
long gap between mountain ridges.

He hoped the combatants had simply called a halt
because of nightfall. If the Indians he had seen in the
valley returned, his life might well be forfeit before
the sun rose again.

He felt his way forward, bumping into trees with
his outstretched hand; a rifle being of no use in
darkness, his knife was ready in the other.

Someone spoke from the shadows, a young voice,
unalarmed. "Fox Brother, is that you?"

Terrebonne sprang toward the sound, and his
knife sank into flesh. Then his hands were busy
stifling the cry that was rising in the sinewy throat
they held, crushing it to silence.

Was there another here? Or did the youth expect
another watcher to come up from what was obviously
a siege below? He listened again, but only the sough
of wind in the tops of the pines and the stamping and
snorting of disturbed horses came to his ears. Far
away a lone cry rose, shrill and plaintive, and he knew
that a wolf hunted the ridges, but it was too distant to
pose a problem.

Again he moved forward toward the rank scent of
horseflesh. They stood, he knew, in the single grass
patch on this slope, and below it was a long stretch of
scree, fallen rock mingled with gravel washed from

the mountains by years of rain and snow runoff. If the horses were stampeded, that was the way they would go, for a frightened animal usually took the easiest way.

Without waiting for another impulse, Terrebonne raised his arms and shouted loudly, "*Allons-y, mes amis! Hieeeeeyah!*" Then he trampled recklessly forward, bearing down on the cluster of animals.

There came a volley of terrified snorts and whinnies, the trample of many hooves on grass and then on pebbles. Once they moved onto the scree, the horses began to slip, clattering frantically as they half ran, half slid down the long slope toward the cone of debris in the valley.

Standing above, his face stretching into a grin, Jules waited, listening, watching, for now, clear of the trees, the beasts were a tangle of shadows against the paler stone. From below came a shrill cry, followed by deep-voiced shouts as the warriors realized that their mounts were panicking.

Terrebonne carefully checked the load in his Hawken, felt the flint, primed the weapon, and started down after the horses, keeping to the grass rather than risking the noise of negotiating the rocky patch. Moving into the screen of young pines that edged the valley, he watched. The moon was now up over the ridge to the east and there was a faint glimmer of light.

Shadowy figures wove among the frantic horses, catching, calming . . . until he took careful aim and the roar of the Hawken shocked the night.

Then there was action, indeed. He ran, stooping, among the trees, found a new spot to reload, and killed another of the attackers, who appeared briefly between the pines. And now he heard movement deeper among the trees surrounding the cabin where his confederates would be holed up. A shout.

"Jules?"

He answered with the whistle that was their peculiar signal. In reply there came the sound of men moving rapidly through the darkness, and soon flashes and the smell of thick gunpowder filled the valley. Dark shapes fell and did not rise as the trappers battled their enemy in the blackness.

This was not, Terrebonne knew, to the taste of any Indian he had ever met. These—Crow, he suspected, though they were usually friendly with whites—were no different from others of their breed.

Within a short time there came an ululating call and the intruders melted away, leaving behind only the stink of rifle smoke and the dark blots of blood on the ground where their dead and wounded had lain.

A huge figure, its teeth gleaming in a wide grin, surged out of the trees and wrapped him in a bear hug. "*Mon ami!* It is good to find you here, when we need you most."

Terrebonne growled as he freed himself from the embrace. Philippe knew he hated being touched, being confined in any way. But Jules was back in one piece, after terrible trials, and perhaps that was enough. He would not require the respect he usually demanded . . . not tonight, at least.

Tomorrow would be another day, with its own problems.

chapter

— 5 —

Spring came fast, though a few late storms interrupted the balmy weather. The grass grew tall on the
prairie, and the horses were fat and full of energy.
Cleve, once he began recovering his strength, picked
up meat and muscle as he pushed himself to ready
the traps and the bales for moving.

Second Son did not understand the ways of whites,
French or American, though she was beginning to
know this new husband of hers. He was shocked, she
discovered, at the thought of stealing, though from
what she had seen of the Fransay, they stole with
great enthusiasm when offered the chance.

However, Cleve explained to her, very patiently

and more than once, for them to show up with what was obviously a couple of winters' worth of furs was to court disaster. "They'd know right off these were stolen," he kept saying, although she tried to make him see that the plunder of war was an honorable thing.

"No," he said at last. "You just don't understand. We don't want trouble with anybody, and in order to make it look right we've got to hide these bales someplace safe and dry and easy for us to find but hard for anybody else. We don't want Terrebonne coming after us, wanting Henri's plews, and we don't want the trading companies looking at us slant-eyed, wondering if we're murderers."

"But I *did* kill that Fransay," she said, puzzled.

He laid an arm over her shoulder, warm and heavy against her skin. Among her people such a show of affection was rare, and she had never known it before. She should not allow herself to be affected when he did something casual and affectionate. Yet her skin crinkled with pleasure, though she never let that show.

"That wasn't murder, it was self-defense. . . ." He sighed and shook his head. "Let's just get a move on before Terrebonne begins to wonder what happened to his second spy. We don't want to leave any tracks, and we want to go someplace where he'd never think to look for us. Where do you think we might find a place like that?"

Second Son gazed off into the cottonwoods, thinking of the mountains she had visited once when she was traveling with other young warriors of the band. Her people did not often range far from their own country, but there was a need to know the lands about it, and they had gone into the Shadow Mountains. She remembered deep clefts down which streams thundered in spring and hidden valleys where beaver worked without stopping to notice passing men.

That was the place for them, deep in Crow country where few dared to travel openly.

She turned to Cleve and nodded. "I know the spot. There are flat-tails—so many that you have not enough fingers to count them. There are streams and dams hidden away in canyons so steep that it is almost impossible to enter them; there are so many that even if someone searched for us for many moons, they could not find us.

"The Absaroka do not welcome other kinds as do Tsistsistas. Fear of their anger will keep away most who might come."

Yellow Hair's face was lighting with enthusiasm, and she went ahead swiftly. "I know the trails, for my people taught us well as children. It is always good to know the territory of those who may become enemies. I can lead us up into those dark mountains, across the hidden passes, and down into the valleys where our traps will be full and we will be safe."

"Then we must go now. I can sit a horse again all day long, and I can hang in there almost as well as I could before. We'll skedaddle now, before the plains get too full of hunters." Cleve tied the last bale firmly and heaved it into the pile waiting to be loaded onto horseback.

They were well fixed for horses: Socks and the packhorse Cleve had brought, Second Son's mare and the young stallion, and Henri's four could carry a lot of weight. That was good, for a travois makes marks in soil that can be followed by a blind man, and brushing away that trail makes marks of its own, besides taking much time.

When they led the horses out of the draw at the far

western end of the creek that had sheltered the
Frenchman's cabin, they emerged onto stony ground
that held little trace of their passing. Four of the
animals carried great bales of furs. Two bore the tipi
skins, the supplies and traps and equipment salvaged
from Henri Lavallette's supplies. Shadow and Socks
snorted and pranced when their riders mounted and
moved toward the west, where distant glints of white
marked the line of the first range of mountains.

"Those the Absarokas?" asked Cleve as they
climbed into their saddles, turning straight toward
the setting sun.

"No. They are between us and our goal. There is a
river, very deep, very swift, and a canyon through
which it runs and where the wind blows strong.
Beyond is a wide valley, but we go across it and up the
edge of the Shadow Mountains to the trails I know.
Those are dark places, where spirits groan in the
night and springs run hot from the stone."

Yellow Hair laughed, sounding like himself again.
"Ma would like that—a place where you get your wash
water hot from the ground. Beats stirring a pot over
a smoky fire . . . but I guess you wouldn't know
about that. Never saw a washpot since I left Missouri."
He sighed.

It distressed Second Son when her man withdrew
into that past she could not share with him. Yet she
was wise enough to remain silent, riding with her
head up, testing the wind for any sound or scent, any
flicker of motion that might spell danger.

Mule deer, flapping their long ears and moving
lazily away from their course, were noted and dis-
missed. Jackrabbits bounded through the grass with
their tails bobbing, and birds flew up before the
hooves of the horses. Sage grouse, doves, meadow-

larks, jays, and high-wheeling hawks punctuated their journey. Her keen eyes even spotted an eagle, circling so high above that he was the barest speck, just visible even to the gaze of one of her people.

"There will be places to hide those furs," she said at last, just to break the silence.

Cleve turned his head as if startled out of distant thoughts. For an instant, his eyes still looked inward, but almost at once he nodded, interested. "That sounds good. Caves?"

"There are caves, yes. Dry ones, where we could bury the bales with rock. But there are always mice and chipmunks and small creatures that gnaw at anything they find. How can we keep those away?" she asked.

Yellow Hair looked thoughtful. "We'll find a way," he said. He touched his heels to Sock's belly, and the gelding picked up his pace. They had alternately ridden and walked, leading the horses for hours, and the sun was down behind the distant peaks.

It would be night soon, and Second Son gestured toward a slope that was striped with outcrops of stone. "If we cross that, there should be shelter beyond," she said. "The stone makes little caves where the dirt washes away beneath them. We might build a hidden fire and cook our meat tonight. Snip, at least, would like that."

The dog, hearing his name, gave a sharp yip. He had followed patiently after the horses all afternoon, and he was beginning to limp, as if a sharp stone had cut the pad of his left front paw.

Second Son found herself thinking of the dog as a person, which was something she had never done before. Her people used dogs to pull travois, ate them, relied upon their clamor for warning of predators, human or animal, but they had never regarded them as companions. Now she found herself talking to Snip when they hunted or wandered alone together, as if he were a fellow warrior.

Now he led the way up the heaving slope, over one shoulder and down the side away from the wind. As she remembered from earlier visits here the shelves of rock strata thrust out at intervals, each making a small porch where weather had carried away the soil beneath the rock layer. Some of those, where the overhang was strong enough to hold itself securely, were deep enough for two people and a fire and even a dog to shelter in.

They unloaded the horses. Water would not be at hand for a day or so yet, and Cleve used a pot and Henri's water bag to offer each of the beasts a long draft. Then they built a tiny fire of buffalo chips, dried grass, and twigs from the scanty scrub.

Sitting on either side of the blaze, they toasted bits of rabbits shot during their long day's journey. Second Son savored the meat, warmed her toes, and took comfort in the fact that Cleve had returned to her side from wherever he went when his gaze turned inward.

Dawn found them well on their way again, heading due west toward the southern slopes of the mountains ahead. Behind them they had left no trace of their passing except for dung from the animals, but Second Son knew that was enough if any tracker cared to try following.

They needed to get well into the mountains, riding up creeks to hide tracks, sticking to rocky slopes, making always for the backbone of that lower range that barred their way to the Absarokas. Though the peaks ahead was forbidding and the slopes and ridges steep and difficult, they were not nearly so harsh as those of the Shadow Mountains.

In two days the white sawtooth shapes loomed large ahead. The horses raised their heads early one morning and snorted. Hefting the water bag, Second Son was glad they had scented the stream ahead, for the supply was low. Only the grass, still fat with water from the spring rains and winter snows, had kept the animals in good shape.

Before dark they were at the stream, but they tied the horses beyond a small hillock, after letting them drink briefly. After the long ride over lands already drying as the snow waters decreased in the streams and the rain of winter stopped, this little valley along the river was a relief. Greenery spotted its banks, and beyond the water the land sloped up abruptly into the foothills.

They slept lightly, keeping one eye open, for Second Son knew that roving bands of hunters might surprise them, even if they camped at a distance from the water and were hidden by the little hill. Again they woke before dawn and left, silent in the tenuous light, making for the high country.

As they went the light came up behind them, turning the peaks above to gold. The leaves of aspens quivered in the cool wind from the heights, and lodgepole pines furred the slopes with a dark mantle. As they mounted into the high country the air grew sweet with growing things and the sky turned a shining blue.

The stream they followed wandered between the flanks of two mountains, which rose higher and higher the farther they went. They rode in the water for a long time, but at last they found a long stretch of rocky slope running in the direction she wanted to go, and Second Sun turned away from the little river to go higher still.

Now the wind was very fresh, still touched with chill from the peaks above, which were shining with snow. Pale blossoms thrust their frail cups from cracks in the stone, and fronds of green trailed over boulders as they climbed past.

Second Son had always noticed such things, though she seldom spoke of them. Now she turned to Cleve, feeling the warmth of his presence beside her, and said, "Listen to the wind, Yellow Hair. Smell the pines and the snow high above us. This is a good place, but the mountains to which we go are even finer."

He smiled and touched his heels to the gelding's sides. Socks turned to follow Shadow as Second Son urged her mount up a steeper slope, where shale and stone grated beneath her hooves. Even as she watched ahead and behind she was alert to the sky above, and when the hawk circling there altered the curve of his sweep, she noted it.

She urged Shadow the rest of the way to the top of the rocky incline, where it ended against a sheer cliff, and turned to gesture for Cleve to follow quickly. When the hawk stooped to observe a place you could not see, it was best to take cover and see what came next.

A stream running downhill to join the small river they had followed chattered through a shallow cut beside them, its tunnel disappearing into a dark blotch in the stony bluff they now faced. They paused for a moment on a long slope facing the cliff ahead. That ran east and west; the passable ground was a narrow, slanting apron between the drop behind them and the west, ending to their right in a tumble of boulders, on the left disappearing into trees whose tops were just visible, so steep was the slant in that direction. Anyone approaching must come from the west, she knew.

She headed for the jagged boulder blocking the opening from which the water issued. It only seemed to stop the opening, Second Son found, once she worked her way past it. A narrow path of slick rock edged the channel, in which the water had gone down enough to let a horse walk along its side without getting its feet wet.

Leading her packhorses, she ducked to miss the low overhang and rode into the dark cut, which smelled of clean granite and damp. The quality of the hoof-beats changed, echoing up the long nave that ran away under the mountainside. Behind her, as she went deeper into the darkness, she heard the hollow sounds of the other animals' hooves as they entered the hidden space and came along the stream.

Something moved in a cranny, rustling dryly, and she wondered if the weather had warmed enough to allow rattlers to become active at those heights. Ahead there came an echoing *sploosh*, as if something heavy had fallen into the water.

She paused again, waiting for further sounds. Nothing could be heard except the breathing of the horses, Snip's panting, the whisper of water on stone, and the steady beat of her own heart.

Then the space opened out about her. The faint glimmer from the opening, now far behind, could not light the way, but the feeling of pressure lessened in her ears and on her skin, telling her that now she rode into a large room under the mountain. It was a good place to hide from whatever was coming.

She called softly, "We will stop here and hobble the horses."

Cleve's grunt of assent was quiet, and the hooves stopped. She slid down from Shadow's back and led the mare to the nearest wall, picking her way carefully to avoid stumbling over rocks.

The floor was perfectly smooth and still damp. Evidently this was an underground pool, filling in the spring as the stream carried off snowmelt from above that found its way into the gut of the mountain and emptying as the year progressed.

She gentled the mare, led the three packhorses up, and calmed their snorts of dismay at finding themselves in such an unlikely situation, while she waited for Cleve to join her. Once they had the horses settled, content with plenty of water, if no forage, the pair of them moved back toward the entrance to the cave.

Beside them, the water slid soundlessly along its slick channel, without a gurgle or a bubble. Ahead, the spot of light grew larger as they moved toward it. When they arrived at the bastion of rock that, from the outside, looked as if it blocked further entry into the hole, they crept on hands and knees, out of sight against the darkness of the tunnel.

Lying flat beside Cleve on the chilly stone, Second Son listened for the hawk. Its *skree* echoed outside the cave, bouncing off the mountain beyond the ravine. It might be that the hawk had seen a puma or a bear. But it might also be that men moved up that abrupt slope to the west, heading for the path they had climbed. That was the only good route down to the river from this particular ridge. Whoever might be coming, it was better to be cautious than to regret your carelessness.

The sun slanted into the cranny, warming the stone, making her feel relaxed and sleepy. Second

Son propped her chin on a rock and kept her gaze fixed on a point past which anyone approaching from the western end of this route would have to come. Waiting was a thing her people knew well.

There was the feeling of intrusion running through her. Others moved along this high stretch, and in these mountains they would be far more likely to be enemies than friends. In spring it might be almost any of several bands of a number of tribes.

Beside her, Cleve stretched out his hand and touched her shoulder. He squeezed gently and pointed, keeping his arm low to the rocky floor.

Something moved in the shadows beyond the bright patch of sun on stone. A horse came into view, the sound of its hooves a tiny clatter in the distance. On its back was a warrior whose black-and-white-striped face seemed like that of a spirit in the strong light into which he rode. A scarlet line jagged down his chest, and he held in his free hand a rifle with a clutch of feathers bound to its barrel. They fluttered in the wind that blew down the canyon.

She did not move, freezing to the stone like a lizard as the rider drew nearer, his course slanting down along the same route they had taken. Would he see the traces where the horses had slipped among the stones? Would he check the cave along the creek? Did he know the boulder was a screen rather than a barrier?

Second Son moved silently, stringing her bow in the shadow of the great rock, laying her quiver of arrows beside her. Cleve, as silently, was loading and priming the Frenchman's musket. But they were not eager to do battle here, for other riders followed the first, six of them in single file. One was obviously not Absaroka, as the rest clearly were.

He was a white man, his tattered deerhide vest marked with streaks of dried blood, his face livid and lined with dark bruises. One arm was held crookedly against his side, and he winced as the horse moved, as if the motion pained him.

She heard Cleve draw a careful breath beside her, and she knew that his instinct would be like hers, if this rider had been one of her own band. He would want to retrieve that white man, French or American, if it could be done.

She had no such desire, for her experience of the Fransay had not been pleasant. She laid a quieting hand on his arm and they watched as the troop began to descent.

There was a flurry of motion, horses milling, and one, a gray, broke from the line and tore toward the shadow in which they hid. It was the white man, guiding his horse with his knees, his useless arm flapping, his other hand evidently bound to his saddle.

He made for the runnel, and Second Son slipped behind the shielding boulder while Cleve stepped down into the channel, up to his waist in icy water, to let the horse scramble past him into the cave.

Once the horse pounded past, they came out of hiding and opened fire on the pursuing Crow. The whiz of her arrows was punctuated by the roar of the musket, which Cleve reloaded and fired faster than anyone she had ever seen using that noisy weapon.

Peering through a cranny, Second Son checked on the warriors outside. One lay twitching, just outside the cut, and the rest had gone to earth, their horses taking shelter along the cliff, out of range of fire from the cave. For the moment there was nothing to shoot at, and she turned her attention to the stranger, who was leaning over, biting at the throng securing his hand to his saddlebow.

Cleve was standing beside him, his knife out. "Let me do that," he said.

The skinny back straightened, and she got her first good look at the newcomer. Above the blood and dirt, she saw colorless eyes in a narrow skull. The jawline was sharp, the flat cheeks lined, but there was a look of wonder on his face that reminded her of a baby seeing something new and wonderful.

"May the Lord bless you," said the man, his voice cracked and thin. "But how did you come to be here in the bowels of the earth, just when I needed you?"

"You're American," said Cleve. "From Missouri, or I'm not standing here."

"Grand Roche," he said. "On the Miss'ssippi. You?"

"Just a farm along the Little Sac. Here, I'll help you down." Cleve reached to lift the thin shape from the horse as easily as if the man had been a child.

The escapee sagged against him, as if the last of his strength had drained away. But Second Son turned again, hearing movement, and sent an arrow toward a dark spot moving against the pale stone. The Crow were creeping toward the cranny, hoping to recover one prisoner and take more, she knew.

"Lay him down and load your weapon," she said to Cleve in their mixture of languages. "It is time to count coup upon the Absaroka."

"Here, I can shoot, too, even one-handed," said the man. "Nobody can say that Holy William is any quitter, whatever happens. Hand me a shooter, will you, boy?"

While Second Son kept Crow heads down with a careful sequence of shots, Yellow Hair loaded the second rifle they had taken from Henri. Then they all crawled to what points of vantage they could locate, few and crowded though those might be in this constricted place, and began picking off anything that rose above the pale gray granite of the slope.

Second Son knew that no Indian, Crow or Cheyenne, liked to attack an entrenched enemy. That was a fool's game, as Cleve called it, and they were not fools. In time, as the light failed and the evening wind swept, chill and damp, down the slopes, the enemy fell silent.

For a long while Second Son waited, listening, but nothing but wind and the cry of a distant owl and the faint wail of a coyote came to her ears. When no shot had been fired for half an hour, she touched Cleve lightly, pointed outward, and slid along on her belly to get out of the cut. Shadows lay dark on the rocky mountainside.

There were no bodies, for the Crow would have taken away any dead or wounded, but from far below she could hear the clink of an occasional hoof on rock. They had gone. Only smears of blood, black now against the rock and still smelling sharp and acrid on the air, were left to show they had been there.

She gave the whimpering cry of a horned owl and turned back to the cave, where Cleve had led their new ally back into the big cavern where the horses waited. They had a small fire going, using dried grass and dead branches from the brush just outside the opening. The red light flickered weirdly on the damp stone and turned the eyes of the horses to coins of silver.

When she stalked in and hunkered over the fire to warm herself, she heard the thin man draw a sudden breath. "This your woman?" he asked Cleve, his tone dubious.

She almost laughed aloud as Cleve put another chunk of dead brush on the fire and said, "No. I'm her wife." He didn't show the faintest trace of a smile, and his tone was perfectly solemn.

After a long moment the man said, "I'm William Kelly. They call me Holy William, being as I'm a preacher. You two married?" He didn't sound hopeful.

"Much as you can get," said Cleve. "In the Cheyenne way, of course. So don't get going on how sinful it is or I'll be sorry we helped you out."

There was another long silence. Then the skinny left hand moved toward Second Son, and she realized that she was expected to shake it in the white man's fashion. She took it awkwardly and pumped it up and down, trying not to shake him enough to pain the damaged arm on the other side of him.

"Glad to meet you," said Holy William. "The Lord works in mysterious ways His wonders to perform and all that."

She didn't smile, for he sounded very sincere, but she wondered what on earth it was that he had said. The words were ones she knew, but the sense of them eluded her totally. Yet she found herself liking the strange fellow as she bound his arm to his side and listened to his talk with Yellow Hair.

chapter

— 6 —

Although he would never have felt comfortable if he hadn't helped Holy William escape from the Crow, Cleve found himself more than a bit uncomfortable in the presence of the skinny preacher. Battered and starved, the man had been abused so badly in captivity that his wits were apt to wander, and even at his best, he seemed to hold all the opinions Cleve had liked least about his own father.

They left the caves before daybreak, still heading for the ridge that Second Son had set as their goal, which would lead them into a long valley and the western slopes. For a long while Kelly said nothing, but at last he began making comments and asking occasional questions.

Second Son, who seemed to have little interest in understanding any white man other than Cleve, ignored the newcomer unless he addressed her directly, which he did in a motley jumble of English, Crow, and Missouri dialect. She answered, usually, in fairly accurate English. It had amazed Cleve how quickly she picked up his tongue, but then most things about her amazed him.

Snip was reserving judgment about this newcomer, sniffing his ankle now and then, but not wagging his tail yet. He'd look back from time to time as he led the group up the slopes, as if checking out this thin man who had joined them.

The thing that surprised Cleve most was that the Crow had not been the ones who abused William Kelly. That had been done by several agencies, including a mixed bunch of trappers down in the southern reaches of the Bighorns, and it took some time for him to dig the story out of the fellow.

As the three moved up and down the abrupt ravines and rocky heights, sometimes leading their mounts and sometimes riding, Kelly began to talk. He was still talking when they camped for the night. His story was so bizarre that even those told around the hearth back on the Missouri by the experienced trappers couldn't match it.

"I come out here in 'twelve, I reckon, or maybe it was 'fourteen. Six of us heard 'bout the country from men that followed that Lewis idiot and come home to tell about it, and we decided we'd try her out. We was young, y'see, and didn't know nothing a'tall about nothing.

"We taken off up the Cheyenne, when we come to

its mouth, and trapped, getting further west every season. We taken up with Cheyenne, Kiowa, Lakota, just about every kind of Injun you can find, from time to time, but they didn't bother us and we didn't bother them. Just traded what we had for what we needed and went on." He gave a harsh chuckle.

"We was more interested in seeing new country than in gettin' rich, and I wanted to convert the heathen. That was the main reason I come along. But every time I come into a new batch of heathen, seemed to me they lived better and treated each other nicer than my own kind ever did.

"They might raid for horses or women, or scalp each other when they got irritated, but I'd seen folks in Missouri do a damn sight worse, for no reason at all, since I was a shirttail tad in Grand Roche."

Cleve leaned forward, watching the thin face on the other side of the fire they'd built under an overhang. Over it their fresh venison hung to cook.

"I've seen the same thing," he said. "My own pa treated me like dirt. Even the Arickara that captured me, back on the Missouri, didn't treat me any worse than he did. If they'd killed me, that was just what Pa would've done if he'd waked up before I got away, that last day."

Kelly nodded. "My own pa was like that, and a preacher, too. Big William Kelly, the Bible thumper. Thumped me a sight harder than he ever did the Good Book, I can tell you. But he made me into a preacher, somehow, and hell and high water ain't changed that.

"So I tried to convert the heathen that didn't want to hear what I had to say. Had their own religion and lived by it, which many of our own can't say. Came a time when the Bloods we was trading with decided I was crazy. From then on they didn't pay me no mind, and it was like talkin' to the wind.

"Then I thought about the fellows I was with. They was dirty, foulmouthed, fornicated with anything that'd stand still and some that wouldn't. Finally it got to me that they needed a lot more convertin' than any Injun I ever seen in my whole trip. So I taken out after *them*.

"They beat me till my skull rung like a bell, and Cottonmouth Luke hung me up in a tree, tied hand and foot, and left me there in a blizzard till I most froze my balls off. Then they warmed me up again and run me clean out of their territory, over the Black Hills, up the country, and into these damn mountains.

"They did give me my gear and my horse, I'll admit that, and made sure I was clean gone before they left off chasing. Once I hid in the Bighorns, they left me be and went back to their old ways." He sighed, a gust of rancid breath.

"So here I was, one preacher too young to wipe his own ass, one horse that'd seen better days, one old flintlock with some powder and ball, some jerky, a bedroll, traps, and my Bible that Pa give me when I got the call. I knowed there was Absaroka nearby and Blackfoot that would make life interestin' if they caught me, not knowin' I was a crazy man and not to be bothered."

Second Son pushed a piece of wood deeper into the fire, her face impassive. Cleve wondered what she was making of this tale, so familiar to him, so alien to her life and ways.

Snip wedged between them and laid his chin on his paws, staring, too, at the man beyond the fire. From time to time his tail thumped on the gravelly floor beneath the overhang, as if he were enjoying the story Holy William told.

"I mighty near went crazy with bein' alone. I never had been so lonesome in my life, and even Pa's fist or Ma's scolding would've seemed like heaven, if I could have got to them. But here I was, stuck in these cold, rocky mountains, hiding as close as I could from any hunter or warrior that come past.

"It changed me, I'll admit that freely. It changed me a lot, and I'm not the man that left Missouri ten years past."

Cleve felt a shiver of sympathy run down his spine. He recalled his terrible feeling of aloneness when he ran from the Arickara, naked on the endless grassy plain, with only Snip for company. He had felt rootless, abandoned, adrift on that green sea, and this poor fellow hadn't even had his dog to cheer him up.

Holy William gazed into the flames, now flickering blue about the edges of the buffalo chips they were burning. "Taken me a while to learn how to live on my own. Run into some Injuns—can't name the tribe, but I think they may've been bunch of Nez Percé, over the mountains on a long hunt. Couldn't make out their lingo, anyway.

"They didn't know what to make of me, that's for certain. Run me through the camp, everybody staring and laughin' fit to kill.

"They handed me a bow and made sign I should shoot at a mark on a tree. Bows and arrows ain't my kind of weapons, and I made a hash out of that. Then they skinned me down to my hide, even cut my long johns off me, and they'd been sewed on for the past three year . . . they could most stand on their own, and they kep' out the wind something wonderful.

"Turned me this way and that way, looking at my

white skin, laughin' at my goose bumps, and then started painting things on me: crosses and dabs and zigzags, black and red and yellow. I looked like a circus tent, time they was done. And I didn't have a clue what I'd best do, because these wasn't no kind of people I'd ever seen before and I didn't know what they expected."

Second Son leaned toward Cleve and murmured, "He is not very intelligent, this white man. Why did he not demand a test? You proved that to be a good choice, for yourself."

Cleve smiled and touched her arm, but he kept his gaze on the preacher. "Why didn't you get them to test your courage?" he asked. "It worked for me, though it wasn't really my idea at the time."

"Courage? Lord, boy, by then I didn't have the courage of a newborned pup. I'd been beat to flinders, hung up to freeze, chased over half the mountains, hid up by myself till I was near as crazy as the Bloods thought I was. I'd of run from a lizard, by then, and I was sick as a mule to boot."

He coughed deeply and spat into the blaze. He sounded sick, still, with the lung disease Cleve had seen so often, back in Missouri.

"They decided I was a woman-man, and they give me to a big lunker of a warrior that had three of the meanest wives ever born. He give me to 'em as a slave. God tries His servants; look at Job.

"Before that bastard got through with me, I'd've been happy with a plague of boils. Bein' a woman ain't what you'd think. Bein' a Injun woman is more work and worry and misery than anybody would believe. Or at least it is if you're a white-man preacher."

Cleve shivered, thinking of the frail little man beyond the fire in the hands of that bunch. He'd heard enough tales about the creativity of Indian women at tormenting slaves and captives to give him a good idea of what had gone on. No wonder the little fellow was so skinny and beat out.

"That sounds nasty," he said. The last buffalo chip crumbled into sparks that died out one by one, leaving their shelter dark. "How'd you get away?"

But the dark shape against darkness seemed not to hear him. The voice came like a drone of memory from deep inside the little man.

"He beat me, once they got done with me, when I didn't know how to make moccasins, so I learnt it. He whipped me raw because I couldn't treat hides, so I learnt that, too. I got to be as good a Injun woman as any you'd find, in time. But you'd never know it the way they kept after me, one or t'other of them all the time. Long as I was with 'em, they tormented me something fierce."

Second Son spoke for the first time. "What did you do to him?" she asked in her careful English. "I can hear it in your voice—you did something to escape him, and you got revenge."

There came a chuckle through the darkness, and it sounded, indeed, quite mad. "Why I killed him, o'course. Killed him dead . . . dead . . . dead."

Cleve heard a strange note in the dim voice. "How?" he managed to say, his throat tight.

"He taken me into the mountains to hunt. Made me walk behind his horse, carryin' all the gear, but that was all right, because I figured I was out of reach of them hellcats. When he stopped, he made me put up his tipi, though we was just there for a couple of days. After I built a fire, he taken off into the woods, leavin' me there by myself with the horse.

"He come back carryin' a deer carcass, and he

handed me his skinning knife he'd traded for off a Frenchy and motioned for me to get to work. So I turned around and cut his hamstrings.

"He fell, but he was a fighter, that one, big and strong and dangerous. He kept grabbin' at me, and I hammered on his arms with a spare lodgepole until I broke both of 'em; then he kept tryin' to bite me every time I got close.

"So I knocked out all his teeth with the end of that pole. Taken the knife and gutted him, with him watchin' all the way. Didn't hardly grunt, which tells you how tough he really was.

"He was still trying to get hold of me, but I cut all his tendons, and he couldn't even flop. He wiggled all over that little clearing after me, and I had to cut his throat before he quit. He taken a lot of killing, that one. I still got his head with me, right here in my possibles bag."

There came the sound of a hand patting leather, and Cleve reached to take Second Son's hand, there in the dark. Even her steely nerves were tense and quivering, her fingers tight about his own.

"You've got his head—right there with you?" Cleve managed to sound calm, though he wondered just how crazy this preacher might be and how dangerous he might prove to those around him.

"Funny thing—nobody never taken my bag away from me again after I stuck that head in there. Not even the Crow you helped me get away from. They taken one peek inside, squinched up their eyes, and pulled the string tight again. It hasn't smelled bad for a long time, so it wasn't that. Maybe they just got no belly for dead men's heads. Or it might be they didn't like the way I decorated it."

Second Son's voice was a whisper in the night. "Decorated?"

"Why yes. I sewed the eyes together with sinew and beads off his leggin's. I sewed the mouth up after I stuffed it with little rocks. Did it just as neat, the way the women had showed me.

"Painted him all the colors they'd painted me when they caught me, red and yellow and black, out of his paint bag. Come daylight you can look at him. He's a piece of art now. For a ugly cuss, he come out real good."

Cleve tugged at Second Son's hand. "It's time to sleep, Holy William. We'll be getting into our bedrolls. You rest, and we'll be up early in the morning and head out again."

Only a grunt came from the angle of rock as Cleve stood in the starlight, reaching for Second Son and holding her close and warm for a minute. That story was one to freeze the blood, and he felt the chill all through him.

Together they folded out the blankets from Henri's store and topped them with furs of their own. Then they slept huddled together, as much against the memory of the grim pictures the preacher had painted as against the frost of the high country.

chapter
— 7 —

Cleve had hoped Kelly would forget his promise to show them his trophy by the time he awoke. But there was no such good fortune. As they chewed cold venison left from the night before, he came scrambling out of the cave, smelling of smoke and dirty white man and something else that seemed worse than it had the day before.

The possibles bag, which Cleve had noticed without thinking about it, was made of a badger hide, the stripes dirty now, the tail hanging down like a fringe below the suspicious bulge that—knowing what he now knew—looked all too much like a skull.

Kelly loosed the string about its mouth and opened

the thing wide. Cleve could do nothing but glance down into the murky depths. What stared back at him in the light of dawn was hardly recognizable as human. The beaded eyelids were strangely ornate beneath the glossy black hair, which was drawn back from the forehead in a tight braid. The mouth was lumpy, the stitches black against the dark and withered skin.

The geometric figures sketched over the entire face in garish shades seemed unnaturally bright and the neck stump was a ragged shadow below them. Cleve understood instantly why no Indian would mess with the thing. It had bad medicine written all over it.

He nodded, trying not to show his disgust, and turned to Socks, whom Second Son had led up with the packhorses and her mare. Kelly, looking disappointed at this lack of enthusiasm, followed. By the time the loads were repositioned and the riders mounted, it was getting very light.

They headed together down the long valley at the foot of the slope where they had camped. This ended, Second Son said, in a canyon where the wind blew very hard most of the time and a swift river flowed between very high, stony banks.

By midafternoon, Cleve could see the sunlit cliffs glowing golden on either hand, narrowing in upon the cut, which was marked with shadow as the day waned. The river they now followed pinched together into that canyon, the way beside it uneven and treacherous with boulders fallen from the heights above.

The wind knifed through the corridor with unceasing vigor, and even now, with summer at hand, they were chilled by its gusts. There were occasional small meadows jutting out into the river, where soil had collected about rockfalls from above. There, grass was green, flowers blossomed in pink and scarlet and blue, and the horses ate their fill when they were freed at last, while their riders washed in the icy water and built a fire behind the shelter of a house-sized rock in a choice spot.

Although their blaze was protected, the surge of passing wind seemed to suck away its warmth, and the venison took a long time to roast, even held directly over the coals on long sticks cut from the cottonwoods that grew near the water. They finally ate the meat half-raw and rolled into their blankets, burrowing their heads beneath the covering furs to dull the incessant cry of the wind.

Cleve and Second Son took turns staying awake in this confined canyon, where there would be only one escape route if an enemy approached. Cleve took first watch, resting his head on a jagged rock in order to stay awake, though he lay under the furs and close to his wife for warmth. He kept only a narrow opening beside his ear on the downwind side so he could hear any unusual sound.

He woke Second Son hours later, when his eyes had grown heavy. She yawned, took the rock from beneath his head, and laid her own upon it. Sleep washed over him at once, and he rested deeply, waking only when he felt her fingers on his lips.

Something was wrong, out there in the windy darkness, where the faintest of grays touched the sky above the eastern side of the canyon. There was a faint vibration in the earth beneath his shoulder, and the hint of alien sound rode the wind.

They rolled apart, taking the bedding with them, each folding and bundling the blankets and furs expertly. Dropping his for Second Son to pack with her own, Cleve crawled toward Holy William's silent shape, which was a few steps distant. He shook the thin shoulder, taking care not to touch the injured arm.

"Huh?" The sound was only a breath.

Cleve set his lips close to the hairy ear. "Someone's coming down the canyon in the dark," he whispered.

There was no other sound, but Kelly moved as quickly as the other two had done. In a few moments all the packs were ready, and the horses had been collected from the little grass patch where they had grazed and slept.

Cleve set his ear against the rock and listened. Still distant but detectable, there came the ringing sounds of hooves clipping and scrabbling among the uneven stones along the riverbank. Shod hooves. That meant white men, but that no longer meant they must be friends.

Terrebonne and his crew might be making their way through this canyon. It was late enough for trappers to be scouting for new beaver streams. Cleve was now Indian enough to avoid useless encounters with enemies, and he hoped to avoid this one.

"You take the horses and Snip and go downstream as far as you can," he said to his wife and Kelly. "I'll stay here and see who this is, what sort of problem they might make for us. We don't want company of any kind right now, I think. We have too many prime pelts to be safe. Particularly, we don't want Frenchmen who want to rob us."

Kelly said nothing, but he followed the line of horses that Second Son led, and now it was growing faintly light, enough so that Cleve could see his hunched shape against the cliffs above the river. Socks was led behind Second Son, for Cleve intended to go upward in order to get a clear look at those coming toward him. His horse would have to be left below, and he wanted no chance of his being stolen.

Once his people were out of sight beyond the next bend in the stream, he turned and stared upward along the buttresslike cliff, which overhung the canyon slightly at this point. The river lay in a series of long bends, with tall cliffs on either side of it. Only on the side where he now stood was there room for a path—on the other the toes of the rock ran straight down into the water.

They had camped just past one of the angled bends, and there the rock came out in a point like the prow of a ship, narrowing the trail to the width of a few yards. Back the way they had come it was wider, but here those who were coming would have to bunch up. If he could get up high, he might be able to see some way for stopping them.

He felt around for a likely spot to climb. After a bit he thought he saw the faint shadows of notches where rocks had fallen off the beaklike stone to litter the narrow track below.

He hitched up his shoulder thong, which held Henri's best long knife, a throwing hatchet, and his possibles bag. Over his other shoulder was his bow with its arrows tied tightly to it. Shooting down with a bow was chancy work, but he might be glad he had it. This left his hands free, and he reached up along the angle of stone leaning out over him and found a handhold.

His moccasined foot felt for a notch, found purchase, and Cleve heaved himself upward, holding desperately, to find another hold, another footrest. Like a lizard, he clung to the rock, his fingers slipping occasionally on patches of damp, his body growing hot with exertion, even though the wind eddying around the angle of the bluff buffeted him every time he caught its full blast.

It seemed a very long while, but before the sky was fully light, he had reached a point halfway up the height. Below him the river had shrunk to the dimensions of a brook, and above him at least two or three hundred feet loomed between his position and the top of the canyon. He found a perch on a boulder that bulged outward from the cliff's face.

It was fairly solid underfoot, lying on a slant of rubble, and behind it the notch from which it had originally leaned offered shelter from the wind. Now he had topped the bastion extending toward the river and he could see downstream for at least a quarter of a mile. He could conceal himself from below and above in that shallow indentation, though that meant holding his weight at a torturing angle. It was not a cave but a dimple in the face of the cliff, and he hoped he wouldn't have to try to hide himself inside it.

He turned to stare after his companions and spotted the tiny shape of Kelly, just going out of sight around a bend upriver. He maneuvered himself about cautiously and looked toward the intruders. In the distance he saw a black horse, so tiny it seemed a toy, moving gingerly over the debris between the cliff's edge and the stream.

Behind that one, there were more, and he counted as they came into view around that farther bend. Two—three—four—five—six—seven.

Some of the mounts must be shod, for he caught the occasional ring of metal on stone, but their riders were not white men. Above the rush of the river and the soft booming of the wind, he now heard the sounds of their passing. This was a war party that had, sometime in the recent past, had a profitable brush with whites, and that did not bode well for Cleve's own group.

They looked like Blackfoot to him, and those people had no reason to love him, though he hoped they didn't really know who had been involved in that battle beneath the shadow of the Bad Gods' Tower. Even as he thought that, from high above him on the canyon's rim came the cry of a coyote. A two-legged one, it was clear now to his Cheyenne-trained ear.

"*Yip-yip-yip-youuuuu!*" came the cry. The signal to those in the depths told them, he was sure, that quarry had been spotted downstream. He listened intently, pulling back into his notch to shut away the sound of the wind singing past his ears.

Again the cry came, farther along now. The scout was keeping an eye on the party that would now be the prey of the Blackfoot war band. Cleve clambered around behind the buttress, out of sight of the mounted men approaching in the distance, and looked up again. Above his perch the cliff slanted backward more deeply, its face pitted with shelves and slots left by falling rock.

This would be an easier climb than the one he had made up the inward-leaning part below. If he could gain the rim, he could walk securely as he tried to locate a good spot for attacking the band from above. Again he settled his weapons and began to climb, his hands chilled numb in the wind.

From time to time pebbles slid away behind him and clattered down the cliff. He froze, always, but the man above on the rim of the canyon seemed to have moved too far to hear any sounds from the depths. Those upstream were still too distant to hear because of the incessant singing of the wind through the rocky passage.

The sky was silver blue in the west, turning rosy in the east. He pushed his head cautiously over the rim, concealed from any observer by a tumble of brush. Once he had done whatever it was he could find to do, he would climb to the top and move down to join his wife and Holy William. This was his bolt hole, which his old friend Emile had told him always to locate.

The plain stretched away from horizon to horizon, as if no chasm yawned below. Empty, quiet except for the morning chirring of insects, it offered no immediate threat that he could sense. The scout must have passed out of sight and hearing.

Reassured, he slithered over to the edge and glanced down the cliff to see if the boulder he had chosen would be suitable for what he had in mind. From where he lay, it looked promising, though he would have to climb back down that steep way to get there. It would be helpful to have a line, for going down was not as secure as climbing up.

Cleve unwound a length of thong that he took from his possibles bag and secured one end to a tooth of stone that thrust upright from the rock of the cliff top. That might give him a bit more security as he went down. He dropped the line softly down the incline.

It almost reached the big boulder, and he kept it at his shoulder, tucked beneath his arm in a loop as he went down. Knowing it was there steadied him, though he knew the leather would be too frail to hold his weight if he actually fell. With regret he let it go at last and dropped onto the top of the great stone, which rocked gently beneath his weight.

Good. The thing was not nearly as well anchored as it might have been.

The riders were still some distance from the place up which he had climbed, and they seemed in no hurry. They knew, for he had heard the scout's signal, that a party was ahead. Evidently they felt certain that their quarry didn't know they were coming. That was good.

Cleve shrank into a knot as they neared, for the sky was growing light, silhouetting the ragged teeth of stone against the pewter sky. Trickles of warm light ran down the rockface behind him, picking out every irregularity.

He had observed the situation closely, and it was one he thought would work to his advantage. Just below his boulder was a long tumble of scree. Other huge stones jostled together in a heap, protected from above by the one on which he stood. That seemed to be less than halfway buried in the face of the cliff. It would not be impossible to dislodge it, given some luck and the grit to risk falling with the slide he set off.

He inspected the narrow layer of clay soil and rock holding the boulder in place. There was a long, jagged line in the sandstone, where weather had frozen and thawed for ages, cracking the cliff apart. He could work this boulder loose, using its own rocking motion to help, if he could only find another spot to leap to once it began to go.

If he went down that long way with a rockslide, he'd end up as ground meat. He had a lot of living to do before he was ready for that.

There was a ledge some six or eight feet off to his left as he faced the cliff, standing on his narrow angle of security. He gauged the jump, flexed his legs. He could do it, he thought, if his life depended on it. Which, of course, it would.

The clay beyond the crack was still soft from the last of the winter runoff. Cleve took his hatchet and scraped away all he could, revealing several deeply notched cracks into which he could insert the long handle of the tool.

The sounds of hooves and voices from below were growing clear now, and he wondered with sudden desperation if he had allowed himself enough time to do the task required. But he didn't allow the thought to distract him.

He chose the middle notch and stuck the tough wood of the handle in deep, wiggling it experimentally. The boulder quivered faintly, his moccasined feet feeling the motion that his eyes could not detect.

He listened past the whimper of the wind for the sounds made by those unknown enemies. The hoof thuds were louder now, nearer. He heaved hard on the handle, keeping one eye on his refuge, should the boulder begin to give too easily.

That was not a problem. The thing was much harder than he had expected, the boulder proving capable of rocking without growing much looser. He worked along the crack, levering the stone with the ax handle, avoiding pressure that might snap the seasoned ash wood. The stone beneath his feet sagged minimally. He wiped sweat from his forehead with one wrist and kept digging, prying, heaving.

Cleve was loosening everything he could, now frantic enough to risk sending the boulder downward beneath him. The thing shifted, shifted a bit more, the heavy end beginning to slip against the debris beneath it.

Now the ring of metal or rock rose above the wind,

and he could hear guttural comments from the riders who would all too soon come into range of his trap. With the strength of desperation, Cleve put his heel on the handle of the hatchet and dropped all his weight onto it.

There was a gritting, sucking sound. He snatched the ax from the crevice and leaped frantically for the perch he had located. The boulder dropped from beneath his feet, changing his balance, and he knew for a heart-stopping moment that he was going to miss his goal.

His right hand grabbed at the other stone, scrabbling to find a grip. His left chopped the hatchet's head over the farther edge, bringing him to a stop. He clung there, his face buried against the rock, while the thunder of the slide he had caused built to a roar below him.

Dust rose, almost suffocating him, and he heard the grating grumble of many tons of rock descending into the gulf below. Clatters of rubble, the thunder of debris into water deafened him; shouts of men and shrieks of horses echoed up and down the canyon like a chorus of demons.

When the bedlam had died to occasional trickles of gravel and grit and widely spaced thumps of late-falling stones, he pulled himself onto the ledge and looked down. The narrow path was gone, hidden not only by dust but by a slope of debris.

The river, too, had disappeared, dammed by the rockfall. Already, the deep, swift water was piling against the upstream side of this new dam, growling as it shoved the loose stones deeper into the mass.

Cleve saw no movement of living creatures down there. None at all. Had he caught the entire party beneath the slide, or had some retreated up the canyon when the cliff began to fall?

He looked up. The way he had come was no longer there, and above his present position there was a sheer face, slick and polished by weather, that wouldn't lend a toehold to a fly. He was stuck here, unless he could manage to make it down the sheer wall beneath him to the upper slope of the slide. That was suicidal, at best.

Without much hope, he gave the call of a hunting hawk, shrill and thin in the morning air. Second Son might hear. And if she heard, she would come, though there was little, he thought, that she could do to help him.

chapter

— 8 —

Although she had been mated with Yellow Hair for only a couple of moons, Second Son had learned that he needed to take the lead in matters that he felt competent to handle. So, though she disliked going down the canyon without him, she led the string of packhorses away in the darkness, moving very slowly, for if an animal were to break a leg among the tumbled rocks, it would slow them badly.

She felt uneasy, having Holy William riding behind her, but after his story she felt that he would have no desire to fall into the hands of any strangers, white or red, at this time in his life. So she forged forward, feeling Shadow hesitate, step, hesitate, step, as the mare figured out the rough route she must take.

They passed a narrow place where a rockfall had almost reached to the stream. She had to lead the packhorses, one by one, past that, but then the riverbank widened enough to allow her to make better time. Light filled the sky, and the first rosy color touched the western cliff tops at last, finding her still too near those approaching riders, whoever they were.

She remembered the rocky ford where another stream ran down from the cliff into the river. Her own people, back when she was a young warrior, had come this way, and they had followed it up to find a hidden nook where they camped. It led, she had found when she explored it, to a rockface that would probably be climbable to the top of the height.

She went on reluctantly but steadily, hoping that those behind didn't know there was anyone else in the canyon, although her own people always sent a scout along each cliff top to keep an eye for such intrusions. For that reason, she kept her bow strung, laid across her mare's neck with arrows ready. No attack would find her unprepared.

The wind sang harshly in her ears, and the river muttered and grumbled among the boulders lining its bed. She kept her ears tuned to anything that might occur to the rear, for surely Cleve was going to do something to stop those warriors who were coming down the canyon.

A deep grumbling sound came from behind, and the ground shook so that her party had to stop and wait for it to subside. She stared back at Kelly, and he shrugged, his shoulders sharp in the morning light. Rumbles, shocks as heavy stones struck the earth and made it tremble beneath her feet joined together with a sound that might be men's voices crying out in death.

The river's voice changed, the flow lessening and the noise increasing as more and more rocks emerged from the depths, forcing the water to swirl around their curves before running on downstream.

She tilted her head, listening to echoes of thuds and clatters that rioted down the canyon. For many moments that was all she could hear.

Then, faintly and yet distinctly, she heard the shriek of a hawk. She loosed Shadow's rein and motioned to Kelly to remain where he was while she dropped behind a column of rock that blocked the wind's noise.

Again there came that faint cry. By now she knew the distinctive way Cleve made the hawk call of distress, and there was no mistaking his technique. He was in trouble.

She worked her way among the snorting, stamping packhorses to Kelly's side. "You wait here with the horses. They need to rest, and I must go back. Yellow Hair needs me." There was no room for argument in her tone.

Holy William looked at her, his pale eyes colorless in the early light. He shook his head doubtfully, but he made no objection.

She could tell by his expression that he did not know what to make of her, for she knew herself to be unlike all other women she knew. She had seen his side glances as they sat about campfires and knew that he had argued with Cleve, at times when he thought her out of earshot, about "taking up with an Injun squaw."

The white man's contemptuous term made her angry, but she understood control as few whites ever learned it. Now she looked into his eyes, commanding his will. "Care for the horses. Protect the furs. If you do well, you may share in the trading. But for now I must go."

He said nothing as she turned and ran at top speed, not wanting the burden of protecting a horse's fragile legs, up the littered stream bank toward the source of the call. She covered the ground swiftly, for now she could see where her moccasins would land, and soon she found herself making the sharp angle that would lead to the narrows she recalled so well.

But there was no longer even a coyote track along the river. The water was becoming very shallow, for a dam of rock and clay filled the cleft from cliff to cliff; a long slope of debris went away up the western side almost to the top. A great chunk of the cliff had fallen into the river, stopping the trail . . . covering the band behind them?

She shaded her eyes and stared up. Cleve had done this, she knew. There was no sign of a man or a horse anywhere, and once she clambered over the tricky footing to reach the spine of the slide, she saw that no one remained beyond the barrier.

Those riders she heard in the predawn hour were gone as if they had never been. No warrior she had ever known had wiped out an entire party, though this was much different from counting coup. It was, however, done in protection of family, and that, too, was an honorable thing.

She lay back against a stony support and scanned the area above the slide, her gaze checking off every possible point where a man might take refuge. The hawk shrilled almost above her, the sound blastingly loud in the narrow cut.

She homed in on it and there he was, a minute figure perched on something all but invisible.

Above him, on the rim of the cliff, was a dark dot that had to be the scout sent by those vanished riders. She nocked an arrow and pulled the bow to its limits, then sent the shaft toward a pale blot of stone beside Cleve.

It didn't reach its mark, but when it struck, raising a faint puff of dust, he moved, looking down. By his sudden stillness she knew he had seen her.

She gestured desperately toward the warrior, who was now crouching on the rim, observing the stranded man. Cleve might be vulnerable to a shot from above, for he had no room to move, no large projection behind which to shelter, though there was a shallow notch behind him into which he might cram his bulk.

Though she knew he must have taken his own bow with him as he climbed, there was no room on his cramped perch for drawing it. The distance was too great for an upward-soaring arrow to reach anyway, she thought.

She paused for a moment, thinking hard. She could do nothing about that warrior on the cliff top from her present position. She could do nothing to help Yellow Hair off his ledge.

But only a couple of miles farther along the canyon there was that sharp ravine where the remembered creek ran into the larger stream. As if it had waited for this moment, it offered her hope of reaching the top of the cliff before that warrior could manage to injure Yellow Hair. It was not far, but she would have to go very fast.

Second Son turned and leaped dangerously from rock to rock, finding the solid ground at last and running back along the way she had come. Now it was very bright, the sun reflecting into the canyon, and she bounded along quickly to find the spot. She arrived sooner than she had expected, and before beginning her climb toward the top she drew a deep breath and whistled the signal that Cleve used when he wanted his horse Socks to come to him.

She had not removed the coil of rawhide line from her shoulders before she set out, and now she was glad of it. If she had to get Yellow Hair off that cliff, it would all be needed.

There was a ford cut in the riverbank to allow the tributary to enter the channel, and she scrambled along that until she was well into the narrow space between the cliff walls. The creek slanted upward very quickly, and she clung to slick rocks and sidled along damp ledges until she came to the pool where her people had camped.

There was room in the little dell for a half-dozen sleepers and their horses. Beyond it a long slope of grass slanted upward yet again, and she climbed that as far as it went. Then it was time to tackle the rockface, which was possible, but only to one determined beyond the point of normal good sense.

Lizards slid out of crannies into which her probing fingers searched for a hold. Small creatures scuttered in their holes as she passed them, and once a chipmunk peered out, face-to-face, as she rose level with his burrow. She saw her own figure mirrored, just for an instant, in the polished black jewels of his eyes.

Then she was beyond him, moving as fast as possible without risking a fall. That would mean that she and Yellow Hair would both die, and she had no intention of allowing that to happen.

When she emerged onto the plain above the river,

the sun was well above the horizon. Her hands were cut, even through their calluses, and her moccasins hung in ribbons on her feet. But she was Cheyenne, able to keep on after most would have dropped in their tracks, and she had not yet begun the major work of her morning.

She stood for a moment, settling the rope, making certain her bow and arrows had not suffered any damage in the climb; breathing deeply, she readied herself for another run. Then she set off at an easy lope up the cliff top toward the spot where the Blackfoot watched Cleve.

She slowed long before she reached his position and lay flat on the ground, slithering forward, freezing at times to analyze any unexpected sound or movement. She saw the warrior at last, squatting on his haunches, his head bent to watch his prey.

Even as she noted him his arm moved, and she heard the whick of an arrow leaving the string. He had only a handful left, and she knew that he had been patiently moving, shooting, and moving again, trying to find an angle from which he could hit the man on the cliff. Given the distance, the wind that would deflect the flight of a shaft, and the angle, she felt that he might remain there all day without striking Yellow Hair, but his presence was dangerous, nevertheless.

Second Son laid her ear to the ground. There was no sound of steps beyond her range of vision. This was probably the only scout the small band had sent ahead. She sniffed, but only the greasy odor of the warrior reached her among the familiar scents of drying grasses and clean air. With her eyes level with the ground, she searched the area about her, finding that the scrubby sage would give some cover, if she moved carefully.

Trailing her weapon behind her so as to keep from making noise, she moved on her belly, wriggling in a silent arc to gain a position near her quarry. She moved around a clump of sage, its dusty-sweet scent tickling her nostrils, and found herself at eye level with a rattlesnake, which had been stretched, dozing, on the sun-warmed stone.

She lay still, her breathing quiet, her eyes unblinking, as the snake raised its head, lazily coiling its patterned folds, and thrust a quivering tongue in her direction. She sent her mind very far away, stilled every sense to quietness. She lay there like a rock or a dead branch, dusty and sweaty, yet emotionless as a corpse.

After a time the snake lowered its head, uncoiled, and slid away into the sage. Second Son lay still for several heartbeats, allowing the reptile to get completely out of range before she moved again. Risking a glance toward her prey, she saw the warrior was beginning to move along the rim, his bow in his hands, arrow ready for the first good shot at his stranded quarry.

He was moving past her now, down the rim. Though he seemed intent on his victim, she knew that all his senses were alert, and no sudden move would take him by surprise. She held her breath until he passed, now only a few yards from her hidden position, and set himself to shoot again.

Second Son burst upward from the gray-green covert and propelled herself toward him as fast as she could move. As he turned to meet this unexpected threat she hit the ground and grabbed him around the knees. Instantly, he countered the move, kicking her in the face, but she moved with his blow and caught his foot in both hands, twisting his leg as she strained to bite his calf. His startled grunt echoed down the canyon, bounding off the distant walls.

Grimacing with effort, Second Son flexed her body as he tore out of her grip; she bounced to her feet to circle, knife in hand, facing the warrior. He was now eyeing her warily, his dusty face intent as he wondered, no doubt, who she was and what she intended to do.

She feinted, lunged, and tripped him as he reacted. Again he twisted to his feet, lithe as a cougar, and faced her, his expression unreadable beneath the stripes denoting a raid that were painted onto his skin. But a tongue of rock extended from a crag behind him, and he was backing away. . . .

She dropped and rolled again, striking with her feet against his legs and taking them from under him. He wavered, his arms flailing for balance, the knife flying away to clatter among the stones. He was on the brink of the drop, the ridge ankle-high behind him.

She half rose and butted him in the stomach, sending him over the edge. He made no sound, but his back curved like a bow, his hands clawing at her, seeking some handhold to save him from that terrible fall.

Second Son braced herself against the stony ridge to keep from following him into the depths. He had been a brave opponent, and as she sat again, drawing deep breaths to calm her racing heart, she regretted having no time to allow him to sing his death song.

When she thrust her head over the canyon's rim, she saw a plume of dust rising from a spot below and to the left of the ledge where Cleve was now in clear view from her new position. He was standing, clinging to a thick spur of rock at one side of his perch, staring down at the fallen Blackfoot.

She shrilled her own version of the hawk's cry, and Yellow Hair's head came up. He turned and looked upward; she waved, knowing how hard it was to see the tiny shape of a person at such a distance, amid such misshapen formations of rock and brush.

His yell boomed up at her and went echoing down the convolutions of the river gorge. She smiled as she uncoiled the ropes from her shoulders and began knotting them together.

It was time to get him off that ledge, for parts of the cliff, disturbed by the slide earlier, were now groaning uneasily. The stony outcrop on which he stood might be loosed at any moment.

The tough rope slithered down the face of the cliff, which was so sheer that the loop at its end never snagged on anything. When it dangled alongside the ledge, she moved sideways until it was near enough for Cleve to grab it.

"How much rope?" he yelled up at her.

She wondered for a moment what he meant. Then she unreeled the entire length, laying it along the rim, and measured it against the length of her own hand. Ten tens of hands. She moved to the edge and flashed her hands ten times.

Yellow Hair nodded and turned to look down from his ledge. When he had assessed the distance from his position to the top of the angled slide, he nodded sharply.

"Drop it all down to me! I have this spur to tie on to. I can make it near enough. You'd never get me up that drop on this skinny rawhide without the edges cutting it in two, but I can slide down it without straining it too much, I think."

Echoes blurred his words before he was done, but she saw what he intended and rewound the line into a neat roll. He tied off the free end to the stone beside him. Then she dropped the coil, which went down like a thin brown snake, its length making a dark line against the dusty rock.

It was invisible by the time the bulk of it unwound into the depths, but Cleve's end was secure. He raised a hand to her before he went out of sight below the ledge, his life depending on a thin rawhide rope that had seen many summers.

chapter
— 9 —

Somehow, he had known that Second Son would hear him, Cleve thought as he watched the loop drop over the rim, slither along the rockface, and stretch its length downward from the handy spur to which he had tied his end of the rope.

For the first time in his life, he found himself trusting someone completely. Even Ma had let him down once in a while, when she was faced with Pa in one of his rages. But this remarkable Cheyenne gave him a strange feeling of security.

He reached to test the knot holding the rawhide fast. It was as good as he could make it, and he had spent his life knotting broken plow lines, broken ropes, broken shoe thongs that had to hold because there could be no replacements.

The line was a thin one, likely to cut his hands to ribbons if he tried sliding down it and more likely to break if he did much swinging on it. Assessing the situation, Cleve, feeling the ledge quiver beneath his moccasins, knew that he must go now. He tied off the rope in small loops, one every three feet or so. It would shorten the line, but it would allow his battered hands a firm grip and his seeking toes purchase as he went down. It wasn't going to be easy or painless, but maybe he could get down to that tumble of rock and dirt without falling to smash in the canyon or being cut to ribbons.

But that first step off the ledge made him break out into a cold sweat. Trusting his life to the line was perhaps the hardest thing he had ever done, for it had to be done in cold blood, knowing what the result might be. He stepped off and hung, holding himself steady with one hand and one toe. Dangling beneath the lip of the ledge, he found himself looking into a cranny that puffed dust into his face as the rock sank back into place, relieved of his weight.

He heard the hawk cry above him and knew that Second Son was sweating this with him. That was a comfort, but he had no time to think of it now. He loosed his top hand, grasped with the painful one, letting himself slide down, his other toe seeking frantically for the next loop.

When your life depended on it, amazing things could come to mind. He wondered how many lifesaving tricks had grown out of desperate necessity like this one.

He hung, a very large spider on a very thin line, above a vast gulf of space. The angle of debris below seemed trivial compared with the depth of the canyon and the wind-propelled river of air that kept trying to push him away from the cliff, straining his flimsy support to its limits.

Cleve kept one foot extended, both to fend off the rock when he swung at it too quickly and to hook around any edge that would keep him steady for a moment of rest. His head was filled with noise, hisses, and shrieks as the air currents sang through the pipes and pillars of stone, their shrillness worse here, where it was channeled into this narrow neck of the canyon.

The rawhide was wet in his grip, making it slick and hard to hold. His hands were sweating, even in the terrible draft that incessantly battered at him, and his arms and legs were as sore as any of Pa's beatings ever made them.

He didn't look down again. He couldn't look up, but he knew his wife was there, her figure tense on the edge of the cliff, her gaze fixed on his distant, struggling shape. He felt caught like an ant in molasses, forever suspended in an alien space, never to escape or to change his position.

Nevertheless, he moved, loosed his grip, moved again, keeping an eye out to his right, where, if he was lucky, the upper slope of the slide would appear, sooner or later. His eyes watered, both from the dust and the wind, but he kept wiping them against his shoulder and turning his head at the end of each abrupt descent.

It seemed like hours or days, but at last he saw the empty socket where some anchoring boulder had been positioned before he levered the higher one loose. He was getting near, he felt certain, if he could only hold on.

Blood had joined the sweat on his palms, greasing

the rope still further. At last he tried to grip a loop, but the hand wouldn't close tightly enough on the loop; the rope was too slick. He shot downward, the rope burning his leg, which was wrapped around it, as well as his shoulder and hip. He almost screamed, though he kept trying frantically to control his descent.

Then he banged against a pillar of rock and was able to catch it with his free foot, pulling himself close, though his hand continued to slip and he hung at right angles to the wall when he came to a halt at last. He stared upward, straining to see his wife.

There was a tiny dot on the cliff top. Second Son was there. He had to keep going.

He turned his head cautiously, trying to see down without making himself swing and lose control again. Thirty feet below, to his right, there was a mess of rock and dirt, a steep slope that ended far below in the river. He was almost there.

But how was he to get right side up again with one hand that wouldn't close at all and another that had so little grip? Cleve pondered the problem while the wind tried to tear his anchoring foot loose from the knob of rock around which it was hooked.

He needed to know how much line was left. That would make a lot of difference. Again he turned his head, this time tracing the dark thread of the rope. Some ten feet dangled below him, well short of the top of the slide. The useless loops were dark scrawls against the stone.

That should have discouraged him, but instead it gave him some needed information. Continuing to slide down would do him no good once he came to the end of his line. But if he could right himself and swing, he might be able to turn loose and land on the slide.

Cleve laughed, his mouth dry. If he reached it, and if he didn't break anything vital when he landed, and if the wind didn't blow him too far and send him down into the rocky jumble beyond the slope, he might just make it.

He forced his agonized hands to shut while he unwound himself from the rope and hung against the cliff, now able to hold some of his weight on a foot that rested on top of that handy knob. He made four big knots in the line, clenched his fists as far as possible to test their grasp, and before he could change his mind, he trusted his weight to the rope and played out the small amount of line until he reached the second knot.

Again he went down, and again. The slope still looked a long way down, but he was near the end of the rope now. It was jump or hang there and rot. Cleve started swinging, pushing with his feet against the cliff to start moving against the wind. After that short swing, the blast pushed him in the direction he wanted, and fearful that he might not get such cooperation next time, Cleve turned loose and fell through space, the gritty breeze whining in his ears. His heart was racing, his lungs straining for air. The fall seemed endless, and he knew for an eternal moment that he was going to die.

Then he tumbled onto the hard, shifting slide, small rocks punching into his belly and chest, bruising his face, and knocking the breath out of his lungs. He rolled downward to come to rest against a boulder.

It shook as he touched it, and he froze in place, struggling to regain his breath, afraid that if this went, the slide would start again, burying him beneath tons of debris. He had to find a way to creep down this unstable mass without setting it off again.

He lay there for a long time, getting his breath, gathering his nerve. The wind shrieked about the tumble of debris while his lungs labored to fill his chest, which felt as if it had caved in.

After some time he was able to move one arm. He checked his body over for sharp pains that would reveal broken bone slivers sticking through his flesh. His fingers found nothing but battered flesh covered by even more battered deerhide. Cautiously, he turned his head and stared upward, but he could see no distant dot that marked where Second Son might be.

Yet he knew her too well, even after so short a time, to think that she was waiting there to see if he lived or died. She was on her way back the way she had come.

Before he resolved his problem completely, she would be coming up the canyon again, probably with a horse. He hoped devoutly that it would be with a horse. This day had exhausted every iota of energy he had and had drawn, he was sure, on years to come.

When he could breathe properly, he flexed his arm. It hurt like the devil, but it didn't seem to be busted. He used it to lever himself over, trying his best not to disturb the unstable rock against which he lay, though it quivered treacherously beneath his shifting weight. One leg moved, then the other. So far, so good.

The other arm wasn't so good, but it worked, which was all he could hope for at the moment. The hands—he stared down at them and grimaced. Better not to think about those hands. He wondered that he had managed to feel himself over with the battered fingers of his right hand.

Now to get down. He crawled, rolling as much as anything else, far to one side of the slant of rubble,

digging his elbows and knees into the scree to keep
from tumbling out of control into the depths. Once
he had to flatten himself, arms and legs spread wide,
to keep from sliding into a loose sinkhole of dust.

Gasping with tension, he inched his way down
again, as loose rocks went clattering, their final im-
pact lost in the distance. Their crashes sounded as if
they were a very long way below, but he didn't allow
himself to think of that.

A foot at a time, he descended the unstable rock,
working himself around until he lay up and down the
slope instead of across it. His toes dug into the slanted
surface, and he found that stabilized him enough to
take the worst pressure off his painful hands.

He had left his bow and arrows on the ledge but his
knife and hatchet still hung from his shoulder thong
Regretfully, he pitched the hatchet away, hoping it
would land on the downstream side of the slide, and
unwound the thong from his back. Plastering himself
against the slope, he cut the leather into two parts and
wound each painfully around a hand, reinforcing the
bleeding cuts and pulpy bruises and lending his
palms some semblance of a grip.

Then Cleve backed down the steep slope, feeling
desperately for every toehold and digging in his
moccasined feet as deeply as possible, making a few
inches at a time. It seemed that he crept downward
forever, his nostrils thick with dust, his eyes filled with
grit, his bones and his hands beginning to give him
some idea of hell.

The canyon grew dark, but there was no pausing
on his precarious way. If things rolled again, he
would be buried deep, and that was the last thing he
wanted. So down he went, leaving a trail of blood
behind him, until the incline grew less steep and he

was crawling backward easily instead of risking a fatal fall at every step.

He had been keeping his eyes shut to hold out the dust, but now he opened them, and a glimmer of light reflected from a mica-laden split of stone above his face. He turned carefully and looked down. Only some twenty feet below him a fire burned in a hollow of rock.

"Hey!" he croaked, his throat feeling as if a thousand blades ran down his gullet.

The sound was faint, but a dark shape rose at once and hurried toward the long bastion of scree. Before he could realize that the terrible descent was done, Second Son had caught him from behind, easing him down the last of the distance to the remnant of the track beside the dammed river.

The imprisoned water grumbled at the stone, and hissing trickles gushed through crannies in the dam. Somewhere a coyote shrilled to the sky, and nearer at hand he heard the impatient stamp and snort of a horse. Bless her, she'd brought at least one mount!

"Come," she said, urging him toward the blaze, which flickered beneath a spit on which something fragrant roasted, dripping crackles of juice into the coals.

Cleve dropped onto the blanket she had folded beside the fire, feeling his legs and elbows quivering with stress and exhaustion. Second Son knelt beside the fire and sliced off a sizzling chunk of venison, which she kept impaled on the point. She handed him the knife, and he bit hungrily into the hot meat.

The hot food helped him stop shaking, and by the time he got a bellyful of meat he felt more human. Cleve sat warming himself at last, hearing Socks's whifflings and stompings above the constant song of the wind down the canyon. He had time now to think about what he had done, and it filled him with awe.

With the help of that broken boulder, he had killed all but one of a band of Blackfoot. With the help of his wife, he had survived the attentions of the sole remaining scout. And with that skinny hide rope, he had found a way down from an impossible position on the face of the cliff.

He almost felt proud of himself. Then he thought of Pa and his constant contempt, as well as the red-glinting eye of that buffalo surrounded by frost that had been a part of his nightmares since that long-ago morning on the Missouri. No, it wouldn't do to get cocky.

Too many things could go wrong when you were adrift on this great ocean of grass and mountains and forests. He would keep his head straight and his eyes open, and Second Son would get the credit. She, being Cheyenne, didn't have the white man's superstitions.

chapter

— 10 —

Once the weary group emerged from the mouth of the canyon and passed a long stretch of arid country spotted with steep hillocks and stretches of sand, they faced a narrow valley, on the other side of which lay a long line of mountains. "The Shadow Mountains," Second Son murmured, remembering her first visit here with her brother and a band of hunters when she was a very young warrior.

It took them all day to negotiate the rough network of passages among the fallen stones littering the riverbank and the worst of the country beyond. Now they stood staring toward the Absarokas, a forbidding

line of black heights silhouetted against an angry
sunset.

Something about that line of dark ridges and peaks
had always given Second Son a feeling of dread.
Beyond them and to the north was troubled land,
where the ground boiled and shook and water shot
high from the earth.

"There are bad gods hiding behind there," she said,
as much to herself as to Cleve. "But we must go, for
those heights are lined with streams and they are rich
with the beaver you seek."

Cleve dismounted, and she heard him groan as his
painful bones and joints protested the move. When
he was on his feet, he led Socks to the sheltered side
of a great stub of reddish stone shaped like that
distant and far larger tower they had left along the
Belle Fourche.

This one was not as tall or as broad, but the contour
was much like the other. It seemed to be set close
against the steep slope behind, but on its other side
there was a narrow canyon whose rear wall was
notched with small caves, weathered out of the sandy
soil beneath overhangs of gritty stone. Those would
shelter a camp from the wind coming up the valley
and hide a fire's light from any traveler moving up
the river.

Second Son had camped there several times over
the years when bad seasons beyond the Bighorns
drove hunting parties beyond the mountains. It was
protected from three sides, and the fourth could be
held by one man with a club, if necessary. Beyond the
campsite a growth of cottonwood hid what she knew
to be a dry stream bed leading back into the mountain
itself.

They could rest here, build a fire that could be fed

with dead brush gathered from the valley, and let the horses scavenge on the scanty grass early summer brought to the flat cup farther along the passage. She would keep watch, after her sleep in the early hours, but here there was little need.

If an enemy had been near, he would have camped here, and there was no sign of any recent fire. Only the dried dung of mule deer, coyotes, and rabbits was visible, and not even a straying buffalo had visited the place recently.

She loosed Shadow and unloaded the packhorses with the wordless assistance of Holy William. Then she turned to find that Cleve had unsaddled his gelding and was sitting on his blanket roll, pushing bits of weathered charcoal together in the stone firepit.

Second Son left the protected canyon and found a thicket of brush not far from its entrance. Before the last scarlet had left the western sky, they had a blaze going in the fluff of tinder from her pouch. When the orange flames began leaping along the wood, crackling cheerfully, and Henri's pot began to give off good smells, Second Son relaxed at last.

Kelly, sitting as usual on the other side of the fire, finished his horn cup of broth and his skewered chunk of roast venison and belched deeply. "Got to admit, this is better than last night by a long shot. That canyon was a bad place to be."

She nodded, her gaze fixed on the glowing coals, where the face of her uncle, now long dead in a distant battle, came clearly to mind. "This rock"—she nodded at the invisible mass that protected them— "overshadows the place where a battle was fought, many seasons ago, between the Shoshone and the Crow."

Cleve poked a burning stick deeper into the fire and turned to look at her. He smiled, the firelight turning the strands of his light beard ruddy. "How do the Tsistsistas know stories about that? It's a long old way from here to the plains."

"My grandmother was the granddaughter of the chief of the Absaroka who lost the battle here. She told the tale to my uncle, and he told it to all the children who would listen to him.

"On top of this very rock, there where it is flat, the chief stood to see his enemies. He went with his warriors down the ravine leading back into the hill and caught them against the blank wall at its end. There was a small battle, and his warriors were victorious, but the old chief he killed was very wise and he left others behind to come after him.

"Wears Many Feathers, the Absaroka leader, died very near this place, struck in the throat by an arrow, and the Shoshone cut out his heart and bore it on a lance before them as they searched the valley for captives and horses. The Crow know how to melt away into the mountains and the forest, and few were taken away as slaves by their old enemies."

"Sounds like they lost the battle, anyway," said Holy William.

Second Son shook her head. "The remaining warriors harried the Shoshone as they searched; the tribe lost only a few to them. Their horses were entirely safe, except for those killed in battle."

Kelly spat into the fire. "When they lost their chief and had to hide out, it was the same as losing everythin', I'd think."

Again her eagle feathers swayed as she shook her head, the black silk of her hair swinging. "The Absaroka remained in that valley, after losing only a few.

The Shoshone went home again with fewer than they brought and little or no plunder to show for the raid. That is not a victory."

She saw in Cleve's eyes a sudden understanding. "This is still Absaroka, this valley?" he asked.

"Yes."

"The Shoshone came and went and nothing really changed at all." She could hear the comprehension in his voice. "I think I see. It doesn't matter who wins the battle. It's who keeps the valley."

"Yes. I listen when you and Holy William talk about how white men fight. There is no honor there, only killing. It is as good to count coup as to draw blood. It is as good to keep your own hunting ground as to win battles."

The last of the brush flickered as Cleve swept it into the coals. The small nook was growing dark, and she sighed and stretched.

"It is time to sleep now. Tomorrow we shall go into the Shadow Mountains, and that is a harsh and perilous journey. But at its end we will find beaver, Yellow Hair, and that is what you want."

He grunted and lay back on his blankets, his body warm and solid against her side. It was good to have one to share both life and danger. And if she was correct, in time there would be another, still, to carry on the long tradition of her family and to hear her tales of the past.

chapter

— 11 —

Summer was already turning the grasslands tan, and Cleve knew they must find their trapping ground, store their captured plews, and prepare for the coming winter. Though Second Son had said nothing about that, he knew she was thinking along the same lines, for Cheyenne were nothing if not practical.

He was not surprised when she turned and began to follow a stream that had cut a sizeable gorge as it ran down from the mountain range. Centuries of flowing water formed the easiest passages into those steep slopes, and this runnel wound its way down at the bottom of a channel that was fairly wide in most places and not too deep.

The horses could keep to the water when the canyon narrowed too much to leave a track beside it, and only their bellies got wet. The furs, wrapped tightly in deerhide and stacked high on the backs of the pack animals, were not at risk.

As they went he heard Holy William alternately coughing and grumbling behind him, but when the preacher went silent, Cleve stopped and looked back. William was sitting still, his horse reined in, his head cocked as if he were listening.

"Heard something off yonder," he said as Cleve turned back and pulled Socks up beside him. "Saw somethin' move in the rocks there beside the place we turned upstream. Suppose it's scouts for some hunting outfit?"

Cleve dismounted and climbed the steep wall of the stream bank, keeping close to the rock and concealing himself as he gained the top. Something moved, off there where the stream tumbled out of the hills, but it was shapeless and its motions seemed aimless. It was the dun color of the numerous mule deer, and at last he decided that was what it must be.

"I think it's all right," he told William, once he regained the bottom of the cut and climbed onto Socks again. "It sure isn't any bunch of men, not even scouts. It's wandering around like it's sick, whatever it is."

They set off again and moved along, the echoes of splashing and clattering of the horses' hooves and gear bouncing up and down the cut. When they emerged, after hours of moving, resting the mounts, then moving again, Cleve was weary, damp, and irritable. The sun was down and only the reflected light from the sky allowed him to see the spot Second Son indicated for their camp.

The red-shot clouds above threatened bad weather, and that not too distant. "Looks good," he said, glancing around the flat space, where lodgepole pines clustered thickly overhead and their fallen needles formed a carpet underfoot.

On one side was a head-high ledge of rock with a shelf thrust out at knee level so a fire could be built without endangering the trees. If it rained, they could spread tipi hides, anchoring them to the top of the rock with heavy stones and pinning them down with others at the edges.

Even as he thought that, a nervous gust quivered through the tops of the pines and fluttered loose needles across the forest floor. The sky darkened swiftly, and Holy William cursed as he struck flint to steel and tried to kindle a bit of tinder, which the wind kept blowing away.

"There will be wind and rain," the girl said. She pushed Snip out of her way, for he was wagging before her feet, every step she took. "The horses must be tethered, or they may be frightened and run. Here that is dangerous, for the ground is rough beyond this place, and they may break their legs."

Cleve grunted and began leading the beasts to the ledge and lifting down the heavy bales, which his wife stacked solidly against the stone, forming a second wall, which she covered with spare tipi hides. He strung a long line between tree trunks near the campsite and led the animals up to link them on tethers long enough to let them browse among the scanty plants pushing up through the pine straw.

With Snip at his heels, he finished the task, and by then the glare of firelight told him that Holy William had a fire kindled at last. Cleve turned back to the campsite, where Second Son had already secured the hides, moving with the practiced economy of motion she had learned as a child while helping her mother and aunt raise the family tipi. So taut was the covering of their shelter that even the eddies of wind around the ledge didn't make the covering flap.

The pines were swaying, wind whistling through their branches and between the teeth of the needles. The space beneath the hides was very bright and snug. Soon Cleve gained the shelter and they had their pot boiling to brew some of Henri's precious coffee as the heavy drops of rain began pelting down.

Cleve dug the remnants of the venison out of the food pack and skewered it on an alder branch, wedging the spit into cracks in the rock, to roast over the fire. He trimmed off the meat that was turning green and flung it to Snip, who lay near the fire, tucked thoughtfully out of the way of anyone objecting to the stink of wet dog.

Then Cleve lay down against the rough wall, eyes half-closed, planning the winter's work. In the high country, Emile Prevot had told him, summer was brief and uncertain, and the beaver began putting on winter coats early. His thoughts were interrupted by a loud cough from William, followed by a portentous clearing of the throat.

"You're livin' in sin," said the preacher, without any warning whatsoever. "And you'll fry in hell for it if you don't square things up."

Cleve sat straight, feeling his face flush with anger. "Second Son went through the ritual, just like all her people do when they get married. She won me fair and square. What quarrel do you have with that?"

"Son, I been watchin' this gal, and she ain't like any I ever seen before in all my days. She's no whore, that's for certain, and I've heard enough about her tribe to know the Cheyenne don't fool around. But there's been no wedding to suit our kind, so anybody comes around and sees the two of you might just feel like she was for the takin', if you get my meaning."

"Like Jules Terrebonne," Cleve murmured, almost to himself.

"Like most any white man out here," Holy William said, spitting a long stream of tobacco juice into the fire. "They buy Injun women like they was horses, and most don't have the morals of that dog there. They're not goin' to understand that this one ain't cut out of the same cloth.

"Anybody thinkin' to add her to their string is goin' to be mighty sorry. Second Son, she don't put up with that sort of thing, and she'll wind up cutting somebody's hide open and makin' a sight of trouble.

"You let me marry you up, good and proper, and then you can show your paper, if there's need, 'cause I can sign my name good as anybody. I'd hate to see a good man gutted, like that Henri fellow you told me about, just because of a misunderstanding. And she'd do that in a minute; we both know it."

Cleve thought for a moment before he glanced aside at Second Son. She wore the enigmatic expression that was natural to her, but there was a quirk at the corner of her mouth and her eyes were bright.

"You want to marry the white man's way, as well as the Cheyenne?" he asked her.

"It will make the old man happy," she said. "We will do it. But what is it that we do?"

"Nothing much," Cleve said. He reached to take her tough brown hand in his. "Just make some promises, when he asks us questions."

Holy William closed his eyes. "Brother and Sister," he began; then he opened his pale eyes and glanced at Snip. "And dog, we are gathered here in this godforsook wilderness to join together this man, Cleve Bennett, and this woman, Second Son of the Burning Heart Band. They been cohabitatin' for some time now without Your blessing, and I reckon it's time we fix that up."

The pale eyes shone in the firelight, and William raised his voice to overcome the thunder of rain on the buffalo hides forming their roof. "Do you, Cleve, take this woman to be your lawful wedded—"

A roar from the heavens drowned out the rest, but Cleve knew what he said. He'd been to weddings before. "I do!" he yelled, and Snip, alarmed, dived into his lap and shoved him over backward.

Lying beside Second Son in the darkness, much later, Cleve thought of their strange wedding. The rain still poured outside, and a steady drip-drip came from the seam between the hides. Another crack of thunder had punctuated his second "I do" in reply to William's question, and a third had followed Second Son's.

Now they were married, and he had in his pouch a paper, torn from a mildewed sheet he had rescued from Henri's cabin. He had written on it with a sooty twig from the edge of the fire: *I have this day joined Cleve Bennett and Second Son of the Shyan in marriage. Nuptias fecit, William Kelly, Preacher.*

He hoped he had the Latin right—it seemed decades since he had thought of those long-ago lessons with Ma in the cabin on the Little Sac River. But it gave it a nice ring and sounded official. Kelly signed the paper without a problem, though he couldn't read or write except for his name, which he printed carefully with the sooty stick at the end of the document.

Now, hearing the rain, which had steadied to a constant roar punctuated by the occasional thud of ice, the thin shriek of gusts through the pines, the drip-drip-drip of water on stone, and the occasional sizzle when a drop landed amid the hot coals of the fire, he felt somehow comforted and relaxed. He'd been raised by a God-fearing woman, and somehow, though he had never suspected it, being with Second Son without a real white man's marriage must have been bothering him.

Now it was official. Even as he thought that, she turned toward him, touched him, and woke. He reached to hug her close, and she whispered in his ear. At first he wasn't certain he heard correctly. "What?"

She sighed and repeated her words. "There will be a little one, in time, Yellow Hair. You will have a son or a daughter."

He stiffened against her in shock. A farm boy knew, if anyone did, that the pleasurable activity that he had enjoyed since his capture as this Cheyenne's wife was usually followed by the birth of a new critter, but somehow he'd never applied that to himself. He was going to be a father!

A sense of well-being filled him. The loneliness that had been pushed away by the coming of this strange warrior-wife was now lost in the distance. The circle made by the two of them seemed complete and in need of nothing more except that tiny one lying between them, too small even to be a bulge in his mother's belly.

He tried to conjure up the vision of the buffalo bull that had haunted him since that frozen morning on the Missouri, but only the glint of eyes through frosty fog was to be found. He was square with the world. According to William, he was square with God, too. Reassured by that thought, he closed his eyes and drifted off, feeling the warm curve that was Snip snug against the backs of his legs.

They went up into the Absarokas, taking care but making all the speed they could. Second Son knew where she was headed, and she moved through scattered stands of pine and spruce, across stretches of thick grass. They followed game trails, when they went in the right direction, and Cleve saw the big cloven tracks of elk going ahead of them as well.

"The great grizzly bear lives in these mountains," said Kelly, spitting on a wild rosebush as he passed it. "So you watch your step, young man. You got 'sponsibilities now."

"We need meat," Cleve said, his tone impatient. "There are elk and deer and woodchuck here. I hear a grouse drumming right now." Even as he spoke a pine squirrel chittered irritably above them and a rain of debris scattered about Socks's ears.

"We do need meat," the preacher said. "I agree about that. Green venison never was a fav'rite dish. But if you go, you be careful."

Cleve dismounted, for it was time to rest the mounts again, and led Socks up beside Second Son. She and Shadow were moving silently across the bear grass of a small clearing, and she paused as he came up.

"We'll camp before long," Cleve said. "I think I'll see if I can kill an elk."

She looked at him, her head cocked back so she could see all the way to the top of him. Then she shook it sadly. "We do not need an elk," she said. "Our packhorses are loaded and can carry little more weight."

"An elk is big, and I do not like wasting meat. Kill a deer, Yellow Hair, or a fat woodchuck. We will be at the end of our journey soon, and then we may hunt and begin making our winter store."

She had a way of telling him things that any child should know without making him feel like a fool, and Cleve appreciated that. For one as big and strong as he, with education past that of many white men he had met, it should have been a thing of shame to have to learn to survive in this country from his wife. Strangely, it was not.

"What would I do without you, Second Son? Of course you're right. I'll go find us a deer or something reasonably small, and we'll cook us a nice fresh supper, and then we'll sit around the fire and talk."

But again she shook her head. "There will be Crow camped along the big river that flows through the valley in the middle of these mountains. Hunters and scouts will range far. We cannot risk fire for longer than it takes to cook. We cannot risk long talk.

"Take your bow so that we will not even risk a shot. We do not need the attentions of the Crow. When we reach the valley I know, they will not come there. The country there is considered bad medicine; an angry god speaks through the stone. The little canyon I seek is hard to find and harder to enter. For now we must go softly and take no risk of having anyone follow us."

Cleve agreed without any hesitation. It was time they had some peace and quiet, and from all he'd heard, the Crow didn't take too kindly to people intruding into their hunting grounds. Once they camped, he left his flintlock with the others and took a minor track up the slope to the left, along a brook overhung with green plants and drooping vines.

In the distance an elk whistled, and he paused, listening to the echoes reverberate from the peaks above. He went forward again, watching the path, seeing the heavy prints of cloven hooves, the dainty prickings of deer tracks overlaying the earlier trace. There was game in plenty here, and he strung his bow and readied an arrow as he proceeded.

The path curved around a boulder and a thick clump of spruce; beyond it he saw the glint of water reflecting light from the sky. Although it was after sunset, the year had moved to the point at which darkness came late. He had no difficulty in making his way toward the water of the pond held by a beaver dam across the brook, which ran down from higher elevations.

Using the caution he had learned from the Cheyenne, Cleve crept near, sheltered by alder and spruce and young pine; against the pewter surface of the pond he saw the silhouette of an antlered head. A buck was bending his neck to drink, and as he drew in the first draft, Cleve loosed his shaft and it caught the animal behind the foreleg, going upward into its heart.

The deer dropped with a sound between a sigh and a groan and lay twitching. Cleve smiled, feeling that it was the best shot he was ever likely to make with any bow. But he was already moving toward his kill, which he gutted expertly, burying the insides and brushing the top of the mound clean before concealing the disturbed soil with dead leaves and brush.

There was no better betrayal of the presence of man than the guts of his game. If they had been in permanent camp, he would have saved the cleaned intestines, ligaments, and stomach, but as it was, there was no time to prepare them for use, though he knew that Second Son would be sorry to waste them.

Relieved of head and legs and insides, except for heart and liver, the animal was surprisingly light, and Cleve shouldered it and turned to go back along his track. As he slipped between two spruces a part of the shadow beyond them seemed to detach itself from the trees ahead and become a shape. A *bear* shape.

Cleve found himself gazing into the interested eyes of the biggest grizzly he had ever dreamed of. It was on all fours, but even so, its head came as high as his chest. If it reared onto its hind legs, he figured it would stand eight feet if it stood an inch.

The griz raised its nose into the air and sniffed meaningfully, as if hinting that he should share his game. Cleve had the sudden impulse to fling the carcass at the beast and hightail it down to the camp and his flintlock . . . but they did need meat for supper.

He whispered, "You know, my totem is a bear. It's a buffalo, too, but the first was a bear. I kilt it with an ax, but what would you think if I divvied up my kill with you? Would that satisfy you, big'un? You think half a buck might fill your belly enough to let me get the hell away from here with the rest?"

The bear grunted in a companionable tone and ambled forward, stopping within a few yards of the spruces. Again he raised his nose, sniffed loudly, and lowered his head to stare suggestively into Cleve's eyes.

Slowly, cautiously, the man lowered the deer carcass to the ground in front of him. Taking out the fine steel knife Henri had given him, he began cutting the meat, severing the backbone to free the haunches, feeling his way with the blade between the locked vertebrae. The bear watched, interested but alert, as the halves of the buck parted, leaving the shoulders and barrel nearest him.

He came forward again to sniff at the meat, and Cleve backed between the spruces, taking with him the haunches. Once beyond the trees, he hurried away from the sound of crunching and low growls coming from the bear, which now was busy with its unexpected gift.

It was no time to get careless. Cleve went down the slope of forest as if the entire Crow Nation, accompanied by every grizzly in the Absarokas, were waiting to ambush him.

It was all but dark when he saw, very distant but gratefully bright, the spark of the fire that Second Son must have built to guide him to camp again. Risky, he thought. But he hurried toward it, nevertheless, with enthusiasm.

No one was in sight when he approached the circle of firelight, and he knew she and Holy William had taken Snip, on his tether, to hide until they saw who was coming. Yelling a greeting in this dark range of mountains was not a very good idea. There was no knowing what unwanted company such noise might bring out of the trees.

He moved through the forest, his moccasins silent except for an occasional crunch of a brittle twig or cone beneath his step. The weight of the haunches on his back seemed to propel him down the slope toward the glimmer of the fire, and when he came to a halt, it was with a great sigh of relief.

Snip dashed out, trailing his chewed-off thong, and leaped about his master, sniffing greedily at the meat, though, typically, he did not bark. When Snip barked,

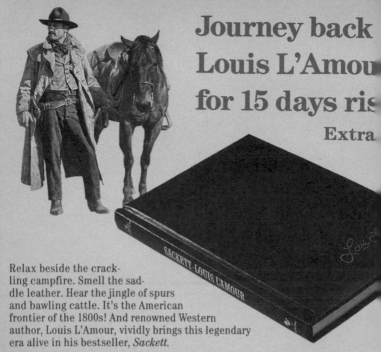

e Old West with
ompelling novel, *Sackett,*
ee!

l: You may keep *Sackett* for only $4.95!*

*plus shipping and handling, and sales tax in NY and Canada.

In Addition to the Free Louis L'Amour Calendar

. . . your risk-free preview volume of *Sackett* will introduce you to these outstanding qualities of the bookbinder's art—

- Each volume is bound in rich, rugged sierra-brown simulated leather.

- The bindings are sewn, not just glued, to last a lifetime. And the pages are printed on high-quality paper that is acid-free and will not yellow with age.

- The title and Louis L'Amour's signature are golden embossed on the spine and front cover of each volume.

you knew to pick up your gun and get ready to fight.

Then Second Son was there, taking the meat from him, and William was pouring him a cup of the tea that Second Son made from the leaves of a wild plant found along the brook, mixed with spruce tips. Snip danced about his feet, his wagging tail hitting Cleve's legs like a switch.

The fire in the open went out beneath a careful layer of dirt. The two led him back into a thicket, where another blaze, this one small and concealed by the surrounding growth and a half wall of tipi hides, waited to cook the fresh venison. They ate standing, consuming the half-cooked chunks of meat voraciously, for the tainted ration they'd been eating had become unpalatable.

Snip gnawed a legbone, growling softly, cracking the bone and crunching. Between one chew and the next, however, he raised his head and pricked up his floppy ears. Dropping the bone, he stood, his head cocked, listening. Then his hackles rose and his nose wrinkled, showing his teeth in a dreadful snarl.

Cleve reached for his flintlock. Snip growled low in his throat, still staring in the direction from which his master had come. His tail was stiff, his whiskers bristling. Then he barked, the gruff warning startling Cleve, who stopped and picked a blazing brand out of the fire. This was not the sound Snip made for men.

A dreadful suspicion filled him as he stepped into the darkness, holding his torch high, and stared up the brook. From the dark reaches there came a snuffling and grunting, and Cleve knew with certainty that the grizzly had not been satisfied with his share of that deer. He had come after more.

Second Son slid off to the left, her bow ready, and he heard Holy William priming his musket, which had been given him from Henri's store of extra weapons that the pair had brought away with them. Cleve laid his flintlock aside and got his bow from the spot where his wife had hung it.

For this work, a single shot and then reloading, no matter how quick you were, would be a dangerous thing, for that was no tender young bear that could be killed with one rifle ball . . . not unless you were more than lucky, and Cleve felt he might have used up his ration of luck for one night.

The griz was huge and tenacious. Cleve could shoot a handful of arrows while loading and priming his white man's weapon once.

Above the tops of the conifers about him the sky was pale with moonlight, but beneath the canopy of branches it was a mixture of black and gray shadow. They were going to need light to shoot by, if the bear charged their camp.

Cleve kindled the shaft of an arrow in the blaze of the torch and cautiously set it against the string, keeping the flame away from the wood of the bow. He shot it into the dark growth lining the path along the brook, bringing from the hidden bear a *whuff* of irritation.

For a moment he thought he had overshot and put the fire into the water, but soon a glint of red light rose amid the layer of debris in the bushes. In a few seconds a blaze was crackling there, and the grizzly, puzzled and afraid, moved aside, around this new danger. Cleve could see the shape of him as he splashed through the brook and came down the other side, angry now and ready for trouble.

But the three in the camp could see him now, and when he came within bowshot, Second Son loosed a shaft, which stuck in the thick muscle of one shoulder.

Cleve could hear her murmuring her ritual apology to the animal as he took his own shot, putting an arrow into the neck.

But this was a big, tough animal, old and thick of fur and hide. His flesh itself was hard and almost impervious to attack, as Cleve soon came to understand. For the grizzly reared now, looking as tall as a tree in the fitful light from the fire, which was spreading into the dried needles beneath the trees and lighting the scene to hellish color.

Snip, who had hung back, dashed forward, and Cleve recalled with sudden clarity the dog's attack on the black bear back in the fort on the Missouri, two years before. This animal was twice the size of that other one and had ten times the ferocity. If he didn't do something right now, his dog was going to be cut to ribbons.

A bedlam of snarling and growling, of snapping and snorting came from the tangle of bear and dog, as they moved in a blur of motion across the blazing floor of pine and spruce needles. Cleve could see with dreadful clarity that older scene overlaid onto this one. Did he have the nerve to attack still another bear with nothing but Henri's worn ax?

There came a pained yip from the dog, and Second Son sidled about, trying for a shot that would not endanger Snip, but that was impossible. William, holding his musket, was frowning as he attempted to get a clear angle, but that wasn't going to work, Cleve knew all too well.

Feeling himself every sort of fool he could name, he dashed back into the shelter and grabbed the ax from beside the wood provided for the night. Then, before he could think of the possible outcome of his act, he turned and ran toward the fight, the ax raised, ready to split another bear's skull.

Strangely, the singleness of his thought and the intensity of his purpose seemed to get through the blur of rage in the grizzly's small mind. The bear disentangled himself, as well as he could, from Snip and stood again, turning toward Cleve, who did not slow his pace.

Another arrow from Second Son's bow caught him on the breastbone without doing much damage but evidently smarting. Then Holy William's musket roared, and half of one furry ear disappeared in a spatter of blood.

The grizzly, tattered and beset by attackers, waited until Cleve was within two paces before he went down on all fours, turned, and hightailed it up the path again, dancing a bit as he crossed the sparks left where the fire had burned across the track before spreading into the debris under the trees.

"Damn!" said Cleve, putting down the ax and sitting plump on the ground as his legs gave way. "I didn't really want to do that again, anyway."

Second Son grabbed Snip, who was bloody but still quivering with excitement, and dragged him toward their campfire to examine his wounds, while Holy William did a solemn war dance, stamping out the blazing lines creeping along through the wood.

After a bit Cleve rose and joined him, and the two of them eventually killed all the live coals they could find. Sitting in the middle of a burning forest was not a thing they regarded with any joy at all.

By the time they were done, Second Son had Snip's worst cuts rubbed with tallow and bound up with strips of soft leather padded with moss. As Cleve stepped into the hide enclosure she looked up at him.

"We must go," she said. "If the Crow heard the gun, they will come to see. We must be gone before the first scout arrives. And that bear—I have dealt with grizzly before this. He will come back. He knows there is food here. He will not be afraid for long."

Cleve felt as if he needed to sleep for a week, but he knew she was right. Behind him, William hawked and spat. "Don't figure to be captured by no more Injuns, Crow or whatever. I been there, and I can't say I liked it a damn bit."

Without speaking, Cleve went out to gather up the horses. It was time to load up and get out, and if Second Son thought she could find her way through the night to that promised valley, he was game to follow her.

chapter
— 12 —

As soon as Terrebonne assessed the condition of his base camp, sorted out the wounded and had them tended, and counted the furs his trappers had caught during the winter, he sent another scout toward the Belle Fourche. They must not lose sight of Henri Lavallette, for he would easily increase their take of beaver by a third, every year in which they "harvested" him. That other man who had taken refuge with the trapper would be eliminated on their first raid, leaving the old man friendless in the wide reaches of the plains.

Terrebonne supervised the assembling of the bales of furs, for he intended to send one of his most trusted henchmen out with them, accompanied by two others who were reliable. There were not many of those, but some he trusted, and they must trade, this summer, for powder and ball; coffee and salt and gunpowder were down to the bare minimum.

He had other matters to attend to, for Jules knew he must go back in person to deal with those who had defeated the Piegan. He would never again feel secure in his mind if he did not. Once he had cleaned out Henri, he would tie the old man to a tree and let him watch while he devoted his long years of experience to the torture of that upstart.

He grinned, thinking of Henri's terror. That should soften him up and make him easier to deal with in the future. No matter how he tried to move his trapping grounds and hide his tracks, Terrebonne knew he would always find him again and take his toll of the furs, leaving only enough to keep the old *cochon* going. One did not starve the goose that was going to lay many golden eggs.

In two weeks he had his affairs in order, the furs ready to go out to trade at the great gathering of trappers and traders set to rendezvous in July for the first time at Henry's Fork, and his six companions picked for a trip eastward. Once again things were going his way.

Spring was well advanced even in the high country when he came out of his hidden valley once more and turned down the steep cut of the little river, heading toward the plains. He approached the Belle Fourche from the north and west, a different direction from any his prey might expect, and came down toward the looming stub of the Bad Gods' Tower just before dawn, early in July.

Leaving his men hidden in the river's cottonwood

growth, he forded the stream, swimming his horse, and came out on the eastern side of the mountain, well concealed from anyone at Henri's camp. His man Pierre, who should be on watch nearby, would know his whistle and come.

He left his horse tethered among the brush and climbed the debris lying at the foot of the tower. Sheltering himself in a niche, he pursed his lips and whistled shrilly, the cry of a hunting hawk, four calls, one call, then three. Then he settled to wait for his henchman to join him.

The sky grew light, the sun running westward in ocher streaks across the greening grass toward the tower where he waited, but Pierre did not come. He could not risk waiting longer here, so Jules turned back toward the cottonwoods beside the river and his restless companions.

The clean wind swept through the spot where they waited, but it did not comfort Terrebonne. They were losing time. They counted many weapons against only two, and if he had been the man he used to be, that would have made him confident enough to ride into the camp without hesitation. Now he waited like a shivering dog for another night to fall, so they could creep in like thieves.

And what of Pierre? Why did he not reply when his master called? This worried Terrebonne more than anything else, and once twilight gathered in the lee of the mountain, he crept out again and began climbing the rock, whistling from time to time, but never receiving any reply.

The moon was full, the sky clear, with only a few wisps of cloud far to the south. The top of the tower, when he reached it, was well lit, the protrusions of rock making black puddles of shadow behind them.

He stared off across the plain, but nothing moved there.

Making his way around the height, he looked down in the direction where he knew Henri's camp must be hidden, but no spark of light showed anywhere. Terrebonne's feet found a passable track and he followed it around the curve of the mountaintop, keeping eyes and ears alert. Still nothing moved, though he could hear the faint wail of wind rising among the fluted stones about him. And now the clean air was tainted with something foul. Rotten. An animal had died here, he thought as he crept forward in semidarkness.

His foot rolled on something and he almost fell, catching himself painfully against a stub of rock. Round stones did not occur on the tops of mountains. They were found in streams, where water rolled them down from the heights, smoothing and curving them all the way. What sort of stone had his foot struck?

He felt along the narrow ledge, which was edged on one side by the cliff down which it sidled and on the other by a lip of rock. His fingers found the thing; not entirely round, it was straggly on much of its surface . . . grass or some such growth. He held it gingerly and carried it into the moonlight.

"Mon Dieu!" He almost dropped the thing, as teeth grinned at him, eye sockets glared with black intensity between remnants of flesh. The lower jaw dropped and clattered on the stone at his feet. The lank hair tickled his wrist as he held the skull up into the moonlight.

It was Pierre, there was no doubt: the same long front teeth, the left one twisted and yellow, and the incisors missing on each side. The hair, as much as he could see in the dim light, was Indian black, and a scarlet garter, gleaned from a whore in St. Louis, Jules recalled, still held it back from his face.

Between the empty sockets a jagged gash showed where something had splintered the bone of the skull. Someone had struck his friend a dreadful blow, there on the height of the Bad Gods' Tower. Henri had been a big man, large enough to manage such a blow.

Jules bent and stared along the ledge, up and down, until he found a gnawed legbone, something that must have been a finger, and the remnant of a well-cleaned rack of man-shaped ribs. The scavengers had feasted on poor Pierre.

He shivered in the wind, which was growing chilly, and turned down toward his waiting men. It was time to find that camp, to confront those overconfident men who slept there. It was time to reclaim his manhood, whatever it took, and to hone once more the pain-giving skills learned from years of living among savages.

Once he had his handful of men roused and ready, Terrebonne did not wait. Finding the poor remains of his friend had spurred him back into manhood, he thought, for he burned with fury as he led his mount up the stream toward the best trapping area he had seen when he first explored the Belle Fourche. A few creeks entered the river, and farther along there were small rivers flowing into it, well grown with cottonwood and willow, which provided cover for a camp.

The moon gave enough light to allow them to proceed quietly up the stream. If it required all summer, Jules resolved that he would find his quarry, no matter how carefully they hid. It was that newcomer who had made Henri so cautious, he was certain, and now he made this vengeance difficult as well.

They found a converging creek very soon, and after directing his men to search other areas, Jules waded his horse across the river, which was now shallow with the dry summer. Once he dismounted and knelt to examine the bank, Terrebonne found that a well-concealed path ran alongside the water. Possibly it served the mule deer, the badgers, the jackrabbits that frequented this part of the river's drainage, but he stood and followed the track, pushing his way past small thickets of scrub.

He smelled old ash before he came to the site where Henri's cabin had stood, and that made him even angrier. If his prey had fled, he had wasted much time for nothing. There was no hint of fresh smoke.

The moon, now overhead, glinted on water where there had been a sort of landing worn into the creek bank. Henri had a canoe? That would be like the old fox, to be sure. But, when examined closely, the grit and pebbles showed no recent track of man or craft. No one had launched a canoe here in days, it was certain. Weeks must have passed since Henri left this trapping base.

Jules built a pile of dried twigs and branches from the creek bank and patiently kindled a blaze. To know what had happened here he must have light, for the moon was not bright enough to penetrate the overhanging cottonwoods.

He lit a stub of dead limb and turned to the pile of ash and charred logs that must have been Henri's home base. It made a pitifully small smear on the green-tan creek bank, and the wind and rain had done their best to clean it away entirely from beneath the scorched treetops that had evidently hung over it.

Now the stone that had been Henri's doorstep was blackened, and the burned ends of logs were flaking away. Tracks of birds lined the caked ashes, and from one gray pile a knob protruded.

Jules had seen such a bone too recently to forget. Again he fingered a human legbone, pulling it from its anchoring layers of rain-cemented ash. He went to his knees and dug with his knife, finding the rest of the bony structure of a man lying there.

That had been a very tall man, and Terrebonne recalled Henri's huge build. This had to be Lavallette. What had happened to him? Had he slept too hard and allowed his fire to escape from its confinement, burning him to death? Yet he lay straight, except for that single leg. The remnants of fingerbones were crossed over the charred ribs as if he had been laid out by one who tended the dead.

Puzzled, the trapper stood and kicked about through the ash. No heat-damaged metal of traps came to light. No melted knobs that had been knives or guns or other trappings necessary to a white man.

He felt through the thin layer carefully, fingering everything, but he could find nothing that he could identify as having been equipment or weapons. Had that stranger robbed and killed the old trapper, burning his cabin to hide the crime?

There was no answer to be found there by torchlight. The next morning even the sun did not reveal anything he had not expected to find. His great plan for robbing the old man on a regular basis had come to nothing.

He stood for a moment, frustrated, straining to find some clue, but there was nothing. He mounted again, turning his horse's head toward the spot where he and his companions would meet after searching their assigned areas. Once in place, he raised his voice in a long cry, which quavered away like the wail of a coyote and yet had too much of the human in its note to be mistaken for anything else.

After a moment there was a reply from upriver. Charrière, he thought, listening to the timbre of the call.

When his people were assembled, he gave the order to camp for tonight. "Tomorrow we will go west again, past the Bighorns, up the Wind River. There is fine beaver country there, for I have been there myself. But tonight we sleep. Henri, he is dead, lying in the ash of his cabin. But we are not dismayed by that, *n'est-ce pas?* We are only more determined to find our own *vair* and make our fortune for ourself."

The grumbles, if there were any, were well muffled, and Jules was already thinking hard as he spread his blankets and lay down beneath the stars and the westering moon. About him the harsh breathing of his companions became regular, and snores punctuated the night, but they did not keep their leader awake.

When Jules Terrebonne had plans to make, he did not sleep until they were perfected. He lay still, silent, his mind busy, but even as he was thinking his hand strayed to his groin, and his breath whistled softly between his teeth.

chapter
— 13 —

It was no fun trying to move quietly through the mountains in darkness. Second Son insisted that no torch be kindled, no word spoken as they left the campsite, which she had tidied so well that there was little sign that anyone had been there in weeks.

"The Absaroka will know," she said, when he spoke of that. "The fire warmed the soil beneath it. There is horse dung that I could not find in the dark and that I could not take the time to sniff out. We have all pissed in the bushes.

"If that one who comes is Tall Crow, he will know just how long we have been gone from that spot. If it is Two Badgers Digging, he will guess *where* we are going. Those are warriors to beware of, Yellow Hair."

For the first time in a very long while, Cleve thought of the comparative safety and comfort of Pa's Missouri farm. So he got beatings. Every boy he'd ever known got beatings, except for the Cheyenne children.

Indians somehow didn't seem to hurt their young ones, not as a rule. Once he'd seen Deer Hoof slap a little boy, and his fellows had turned their backs on him and hadn't spoken with him again for days. But even with all Pa's faults, you didn't have to watch your back for fear of arrows out of ambush, and you didn't have to keep checking your scalp with both hands every few minutes to make sure it was still attached to your skull.

This great West Ashworth had been so excited about was just as dangerous as old Emile had said it was. And he began to suspect that any fortune you found would be the country itself and someone like Second Son to share it with.

Cleve shivered, stepping in Second Son's tracks, keeping Socks and his packhorse on short leads. Behind him he heard Holy William clear his throat and spit, trying to do it softly. It sounded to Cleve like the old fellow had lung sickness, like old Mrs. Todd back along the Little Sac. But he said nothing and stepped softly, keeping his gaze fixed on the shadowy shapes of his wife and Shadow.

They came out of the trees at last beside a wide stretch that seemed to be sand, until Cleve felt the chill wind curl about him and strike through his deerhide shirt. That was snow, glimmering white over the high meadow. The moon, now well down, was hidden behind peaks to the west, but the sky was light enough to reflect brightly from the thin laycring.

Second Son did not strike off across the clean expanse, but turned up a slight incline, keeping to the edge of the wood, where little snow had drifted. Only when she came to a dark line where the wind had swept a broken ridge of stone clean of accumulation did she turn toward her goal.

Cleve guessed they were crossing some high pass that she recalled from her childhood, and he hoped devoutly that she remembered the way. The tame mountains of Missouri had done little to prepare him for these savage heights, where the rock and the wind ruled and there seemed to be no place for anything as feeble as a man. Even as he thought this, a gust came sweeping over the snow, spattering his face with frozen grit and thrusting cold fingers beneath his cougar-hide cloak.

Socks snorted softly, dancing a bit as his hooves struck the icy stone. Cleve walked beside him, soothing him and talking to his pack animal. The other packhorses that had been Henri's seemed perfectly used to crossing mountains by moonlight, for they clipped along over the frozen stone as calmly as if they were on the streets of St. Louis.

From behind there came a quiet curse and the sound of slipping. A thud told Cleve that Holy William had hit a slick patch and fallen; he dropped the reins, knowing that Socks would stand, holding the pack animal in place, while he checked on the preacher.

William was lying on his side, holding his moccasined foot and rubbing it hard. "Stepped in a damn crack and near busted my footbones," he said. "This ain't the kind of travelin' I like best, I can tell you for certain."

"Nor me either," Cleve replied, reaching to pull the

thin fellow to his feet. "You think you can make it across? I know she won't stop here in the open, not if we both was to fall off the mountain."

"Across maybe, but not much more. I'm done, boy, and that's no lie. I ain't the man I was before that big bastard and his wives taken me on, and that's a fact."

Cleve sighed. "Then you'd better get up on Socks. He's surefooted as they come. I'll lead the rest of these and your mare. Here, let me help you—put your arm over my shoulder."

He assisted the preacher to Socks's side and boosted him onto the gelding's back. Socks whiffed inquiringly, received a pat on the nose from his master, and moved forward after Second Son, leaving Cleve to bring up the rear.

He wondered, as he made his careful way across the ridge, what he would find on the other side. Second Son showed no sign of confusion. Every turn she made was as sure as if she had come this way recently, and she never paused to make certain of a route. But he had noted that trait among all her people. He suspected that losing any Indian who trailed him would be no easy task.

He huddled his cougar skin around his shoulders and moved forward, leading the horses and trying not to think. He found that he was weary to the very core of his being, chilled and hungry. He hadn't stopped since morning, and his flight from that bear and what happened afterward had taken it out of him. He felt, like Holy William, that he wasn't the man he'd been that morning. Not by a long shot.

After what seemed hours, but was probably less, they reached the other side of the snowy patch, where the land sloped downward abruptly. Second Son, who seemed able to see in the dark, patted his shoulder to indicate he must stop where he was while she found their further trail. The horses could use the rest, and he wasn't sorry for it himself.

He huddled against Socks, holding the leads of the packhorses in numb fingers. Kelly coughed painfully, spat on the other side of the horse, and grunted. Cleve reached up and helped the man down, letting him lean beside him against the warmth of the animal, out of the wind. He weighed almost nothing, and his bones felt sharp under the hide cloak. From time to time the skinny frame shook with stifled coughing.

Second Son had disappeared down the incline, where a few trees reared warped branches into the wind. After a time she came silently into view, shadow against shadow, and leaned close.

"There is a path down the mountain. It is steep, for we are so high, but once we get into the forest we can follow a brook, and the footing will be easy. It will be warmer, too. By dawn we should come to the rim above the first of the valleys I remember. Come on foot and hold on to the horses."

Cleve handed William the reins of his horse and two pack animals, took those of Socks and the others, and followed again on the heels of the Cheyenne. He was comforted by the thought that tomorrow might see them in that valley where the Absaroka believed their most dangerous gods lived.

They camped for a few hours in the darkest part of the night, allowing the horses to crop the grass, for now they were below the snow line and among trees again. The small meadow Second Son chose was set like a porch against a slope formed of shelves of stone protruding from the steep that sheltered them from the wind. Beyond were the tops of pines and firs, and a thick growth of alders made a screen that kept out all but the worst gusts that eddied around the shoulder of the mountain.

Second Son, who seemed to have a genius for finding spots for building concealed fires, kindled a blaze in a nook set back amid the eroded layers of the cliff, and Cleve helped Holy William into the warmth and settled him with his back against his bedroll. The man's bones felt sharp, even through the buffalo-hide robe he'd been given from Henri's stores, and he shook with coughing for a long while after he was sitting beside the fire.

Later, as they unloaded the bales from the backs of the pack animals, Second Son spoke quietly to Cleve. Listening to her words, he realized that there was a wide gap between them, however close they might feel at times.

"He will die, that one. Our people have the coughing sickness, too, and only the strongest live. He is not strong, that William, and it will not be long. He will be a burden, Yellow Hair. We should kill him quickly to save his suffering, and then we should go on to find our valley."

Her hands were sure on the straps and thongs, and she kept pace with him as they stacked the bales farther along the cliff and tied them down beneath hide coverings. Cleve bit his lip as he worked, trying to find a way to explain his white man's attitude toward such matters without angering his wife.

Among her people this would be the practical solution, and no one would find anything wrong with it. Among his it would be murder, and Cleve had not, even now, become comfortable with the thought of killing his own kind. Many people had died beneath his hands or fallen to his weapons, but that had not toughened him enough to let him agree to this.

"Second Son, among my people we don't kill the badly sick or deformed children or allow old folks to walk away into the snow so that other people can eat until spring brings plants and game. We're taught that of all things that's the worst for a man to do; that's gone deep into me.

"William's not well, it's true, but if he lasts until we get into that valley you promise us, maybe he'll make it. I want to try, anyway. Can you understand that? Can you go along with my crazy white ways?" He turned back toward the fire, which was only a reflected wash of color among the rocks.

She came beside him and slipped her small, callused hand into his. "If it is what you want, Yellow Hair, I will keep my peace. But it seems strange to me; that is a weak way to deal with those who cannot survive. Yet you are not weak. The ways of white men are different, and that is what I must remember.

"I will do as you say, but I do not trust whites, except for you. Two others I have known, and both have tried to attack me. I will watch him while you tend his sickness."

They crept into the notch where the fire crackled as pine cones caught, turned red and gold like sculptures of glowing metal, then crumpled to ash. William lay with his head on his blanket, his eyes closed. The only color in his thin face was that provided by the fire, and he twitched in his sleep, muttering and groaning.

Second Son erected a tripod of sticks and Cleve nudged into the edge of the coals the iron pot that was proving to be one of the most useful things they had retrieved from Henri's stores. Into it he poured water from his waterskin. Second Son added a few roots she had dug among the trees where she tied the end of the picket rope confining the horses. When strips of fresh venison were added and steam began to rise, William awoke.

He struggled to sit up. "Smells good," he said, sniffing. "Seems I feel some better now that I've had some rest." He started to crawl over to the pot, but Cleve shook his head.

"You stay put, William. I'll get you a plate of grub quick as it's ready, but while you wait I'll scoop you out a cup of the soup. That all right?"

Second Son touched his shoulder, nodded toward the bushes, and slipped out of the notch, leaving the two men staring at each other. "Been a long time since anybody did anythin' for me," Kelly said at last, before sipping the hot broth gingerly.

"Much obliged, boy. Can't think when anybody last tried to help me out. I was thinkin' maybe I ought to walk off, like the old Injuns do when they get to be no good to anybody and are doing nothin' but eating up food the younger ones need. But it's summer and food's no problem. Maybe I'll wait awhile yet, if you don't mind."

"You just hang in here and we'll get settled before long," Cleve replied. He reached to stir the simmering pot and to twirl the chunk of venison hanging from the tripod. Fragrant juices sputtered into the fire, and Snip edged up closer, eyeing the meat hungrily.

His master cut a strip off the sizzling roast and dropped it before the dog. Snip, now wise in the ways of campfire meals, waited, nosing the hot chunk for some time before he set his teeth into it and gulped it down.

William chuckled, but the laugh turned into a painful siege of coughing again. When he could speak, the preacher wheezed, "If I'd've had a dog like that'un, I might've come out better. He's like a friend, but not so hardheaded. If he was a woman, I'd marry him, by gum!"

Cleve stifled a laugh. Before he met Second Son he'd almost thought the same. The dog, knowing he was the subject of the man-words, laid his nose on Cleve's knee and stared up at him, his dark eyes gleaming in the firelight.

He'd found a dead rabbit earlier in the evening and wallowed in it with great enthusiasm, but even the stink didn't make Cleve push him away. Snip was part of his family, and his smell was just something people had to put up with. Lord knows, he got pretty ripe himself on long hauls with no time to stop and strip off the grime. If it hadn't been for Ma and her cleanly ways, he would probably have been as filthy as any of the old trappers he'd known with Ashworth's bunch.

Second Son was back, as quietly as if she had never left. She nodded toward the top of the ridge above them as she jerked the tripod off the fire, laid the roast aside, pushed the pot out of harm's way, and covered the blaze with dust and grit scooped from the floor of their small shelter.

Cleve went to his knees, helping. "What?" he breathed into her ear.

"Men. On the mountain. Not Absaroka, but no man is a friend until you know him. Shhh!"

William held his hand hard over his lips, choking back a fit of coughing. Cleve covered the last spark and reached for Second Son's hand, and she tugged him to his feet.

"We go up to see?" she asked, her voice exactly gauged to reach William and to go no farther.

Cleve thought for a moment. It was always best to know what you faced, good or bad, and this was no exception. "We go," he said. "William, you take care. Your gun handy? Listen for the horses, though they ought to be hid by the trees and the dark from anybody up there. We'll be back in a little bit."

After the warmth of the niche, the side of the cliff was cold, swept with gusty blasts curling around the height. Cleve climbed cautiously, setting each finger and toe so as to avoid dislodging anything whose falling would betray their presence. He could hear no sound to tell him his wife was just behind, but he knew with complete certainty that she was. Before he reached the last ledge along which their obscure path had descended, he felt a touch at his shoulder.

Pausing, he heard what her Cheyenne ears had caught before he could detect it, the sound of voices muttering amid the fluttering of the wind.

"*Merde!* Would you tread on my heel, small pig of a Breton?" The words were in French, but Cleve recalled enough of his tutoring with Emile and Henri to make out the meaning.

Warm breath and a tiny whisper against his ear said, "That is Jules Terrebonne, Yellow Hair. I would recognize his voice wherever I heard it. He has learned that his last spy is dead and Henri is gone, I suspect, so he goes about his own business."

Cleve shook his head impatiently. He understood more French than she, and perhaps he could make out what their purpose here might be if he listened closely. As if she understood, she touched his back and sank into darkness, soundless as a shadow.

Cleve went up another few yards, keeping his head

well below the level of the flat area above him. Occasionally the wind sent grainy flecks of snow down about him, but that only served to conceal the existence of this tiny game track Second Son had found.

Now the voices were clearer, and he risked an eye above a tumble of rocks to see the direction in which the travelers were heading. The sky was beginning to pale in the east, and the shapes of men and horses were distinct against it.

Instead of moving across the snowy area his own party had crossed, they were traveling along its level stretch, for that was the easiest way to mount the pass beyond. The trappers seemed to have no concern for tracks they left behind, and Cleve wondered if they knew that the Crow were in the mountains and objected to the presence of others in their country.

Fragments of conversation came to him, but some words were distorted by the wind and some were in French he had never learned. Yet he felt, by the time they passed on, that they were heading for a trapping valley of their own, up in the country that his own cousin John Colter had discovered many years before. The French, it seemed, had known of that hellish place of bubbling mud and spouting steam for a long time before that.

Relieved, he went back down to join Second Son, and together they descended the steep yet again and found their way back to the notch where Holy William waited. Before they arrived, they heard his strangled cough, and soon Cleve had dug out live coals and rekindled the blaze.

Once again he thought with longing of Pa's tight house in Missouri, of the fire that roared every day in the pole-and-cat chimney and the smell of Ma's cooking that hung in the cabin, growing richer with every passing year. Then he glanced up and his eyes met those of the Cheyenne warrior who was his wife.

Reality returned to him swiftly. Here there were no beatings, no curses and threats that he was powerless to resist. When he had children—boys or girls, it made no difference—he swore to himself that he would never beat them if they didn't deserve it or curse them at all, no matter what mischief they pulled.

He settled back onto his bed furs beside Second Son and they ate venison that had almost cooked through before the interruption. William chewed the tender bits of meat from the pot, for the warrior who had been his master had knocked out too many of his teeth to make harder chewing easy.

Snip, who had been commanded to remain behind and guard the camp, came sniffing into the shelter. He got the marrowbone from the meat, which sent him into tail-wagging ecstasies as he crunched into it.

Feeling that bony tail whip against his extended legs, Cleve swallowed the last of his venison and grinned across the fire at Kelly. This could have been a bad ending to a bad day, but they'd missed the worst of it.

Maybe Terrebonne and his crew traveled at night to avoid the Crow, and that had worked out well for his own bunch, for by day they might have spotted that little track and decided to go a different route. All in all, they'd been lucky, even after the incident with the bear.

"You think that griz will follow us?" he asked Second Son.

"Who knows what the Man of the Wood may do?" she said. "The great bear has his own way, and I cannot say what he will decide. The fire may have frightened him so badly that he has gone up into the distant forest and is sulking. But I have seen a great gray one follow a band of my people for days, after an encounter. The Burning Hearts do not like to kill him, unless he threatens us, but he does not mind killing us."

Cleve wondered if somewhere back along the mountain ridges that dark shape was moving after them, pausing to allow the Frenchmen to pass, sniffing the tracks to make sure of his goal. He shivered and hid the movement with a stretch.

"Time to sleep," he said. He bent forward and arranged the pile of sticks so the fire would be easy to replenish.

He woke some time after midmorning when Second Son touched his shoulder. She lay down in the hidden notch while he took over the watch, for they had agreed not to move until late in the afternoon. Nibbling on a bit of cold venison, Cleve went down and moved the picket line, providing the horses with a fresh patch of grass and low bushes on which to browse.

He found a hidden spot among the trees, from which he could keep watch on the edge of the plateau above and the track as it meandered down below. There he made himself comfortable, his bow at hand, his flintlock loaded but not primed.

The scent of pine straw and fir warmed by the sun was sweet in the air, and the breeze, so chilly at night, was now pleasant against his face as he kept watch over his people. From time to time one of the horses snorted or stamped and Snip went to investigate, but always he returned to settle at his master's feet in a patch of sunlight that struck through the overhanging branches of the lodgepole pines beneath which they were concealed.

The sun moved across the sky and began to slip down toward the peaks beyond the small valley into which they had begun a descent. Resting here, Cleve knew that he would get no sleep for a long time, so he let the others doze until shadows had filled the distance beyond the trees and the sky was beginning to darken in the east. Then he rose and led the horses back to the shelter, where Second Son had stripped off cold venison for a quick meal before they set off.

Again they moved through the dimness of a night-bound forest, keeping to the flank of the mountain now, for Crow might well be down in the grassy reaches of the valley and the French had passed along the ridges above. Second Son insisted upon keeping to this difficult but sheltered route until they must go over the pass.

It was difficult going, for the slant was steep, and occasionally a horse would lose footing and slip downward in a scurf of fallen needles until it came up against a tree or a boulder thrusting out of the hillside. The resulting snorts and whinnies seemed to alarm Second Son, for she would leap down from Shadow, if she happened to be riding at the time, and slide down to the distressed animal, catching its nostrils and avoiding its failing legs, in order to keep down the noise.

Snip, who usually ranged ahead and to the sides when his master was on the move, seemed subdued, keeping behind Socks and in front of the pack animals. Even when a horse slipped, he didn't let go with a volley of barks, as most dogs would have done.

The trail they left was obvious to a blind man, even in the dark. When Cleve dismounted and started back to smooth up the disarranged needles and soil, Second Son came back to set her hand on his arm.

"We must go fast. There is no time to hide our trail—the only way we will avoid the Absaroka is to go over the pass before dawn. They will not follow us into the country where gods speak from the earth. Only scouts follow us now, but if we take too long, the larger band will come up and attack us at daybreak."

"But I haven't seen a sign of an Indian. And the Frenchmen have already gone over the pass and are out of our way. What are you so antsy about?"

She stopped; hearing the steps ahead come to a halt, Cleve stopped as well. In a moment the pack animals and Holy William's mount had also paused on the mountainside, and for a moment there was only the harsh breath of wind among the treetops and the distant sound of a wolf howling from the depths of the valley. After a bit there came the irritated mutter of a night bird, well down the slope below them.

Then Cleve understood. They were being stalked by Absaroka, for that sound did not come from human lips. The wolf, too, was a two-legged one, for that howl held a subtle difference from the normal cry of a beast in the night.

"I see what you mean," he murmured. "Let's go fast!"

They did. Urged on with all reasonable speed, the horses scrambled along the slope, and Second Son forged ahead on foot, scouting out better ways for those who followed. They halted only when necessary to rest the animals, and even then Snip kept close to Cleve's heels as if he, too, sensed the nearness of enemies in the forest.

Cleve had good eyesight, even in the darkness beneath the trees, but it seemed that to his wife the night was no barrier. Catlike, she slid through thickets and among boulders, leading her string of men and animals toward the ridge through which the pass cut, following from high above the course of the stream that watered the valley below them.

By dawn they were well up the ridge, among bare rocks that offered uncertain footing. Cleve sent Holy William ahead, just behind Second Son, and brought up the rear, his flintlock ready-primed, his bow and sheaf of arrows slung across his back. He had tied Snip to Socks's blanket thong, and they were both well ahead, moving up the final steep climb to the saddle forming the pass.

As Shadow moved up the track, silhouetted against the rosy dawn sky, Cleve slipped behind one of the angles of stone that had slipped sideways down from the heights and watched the back trail closely. Reflected light now illuminated the upper reaches of the valley, letting him glimpse motion among the last of the bushes below his position.

A warrior peered out of the shelter of the bush before rising and drawing his bow. The flintlock roared, and the bare torso jerked backward, centered with a blossom of blood. The branches shook for a moment with the death throes of the dying man, but Cleve took no time to watch.

From downslope there came a shrill cry of anger and dismay; arrows clattered against the sheltering rock plate, but Cleve had moved past it and was eeling along on knees and elbows among shattered remnants of other landslips. By the time he reached the next good cover and looked back, he could see two other Absaroka running, crouched, up the difficult angle of the path.

Without taking the time to reload his rifle, Cleve

nocked an arrow and aimed carefully, allowing for wind and the downward angle. His shaft nicked the first of the Crow warriors, sending him flat on the rock, and the other sank into some hidden crevice. That would allow them some time to get over the ridge.

He slithered onward until he found a concealed spot with room for drawing his bow. He blessed his wife's nephew for teaching him to use the Cheyenne weapon as he readied an arrow and waited until a dark head, feathers fluttering, came into view.

He drew the bow, low in the Cheyenne manner, and let fly one of his shafts. There came a thunk. A grunt reached his ears and the head dropped out of sight among the stones.

Without waiting, Cleve withdrew again, keeping down as much as possible, for there was one more, at least, back there on the lower slope. Perhaps more, if those he wounded were still able to follow. Even as he alternately crawled, climbed, and ran, he felt a naked shiver between his shoulder blades, as if someone stared at him from behind.

He reached the last steep climb, and he knew he must expose himself to an arrow in the back if he went up that bare expanse. But he could not stay here, and he had no intention of going back along this painfully gained track to eliminate the larger band that must be close behind the scouts he had already met.

Cleve ran at the slope, trying to make it in one impossible rush, but the angle was too steep, and he slowed before he reached its top. His moccasins slipped on the stone, and he almost went backward, as a figure appeared above him.

"Git down, boy!" came Holy William's roar from above.

Without hesitation, Cleve fell flat on his face, feeling grit and sharp angles of rock dig into his cheekbone. From above, booming over his head, there came a blast of noise and a gust of hot wind as Kelly's rifle roared. Bits of powder stung Cleve's neck as he tried to burrow into the rock.

For a moment nothing except the echoes of the shot bounced down the glen. Cleve rose slightly and stared back down the incline, looking for any trace of his attackers.

Flat on a sun-drenched stone, his arms spread wide, his blood staining the rock and beginning to drip onto the soil beneath, lay a warrior, his eagle feathers, still tied into his black hair, fluttering in the breeze. His bow lay some distance from him, as if his dying reflex had flung it away.

There was no cry now, no sign of anyone else nearby. Only the whistle of wind among the rocks and the clack of hooves as the last of their animals crossed the top of the pass.

Cleve turned and hurried to catch up with Holy William and caught the preacher bodily in one arm. The man was coughing desperately, but he still clutched his flintlock with determination. Together they hurried after the horses, over the hump, and found themselves moving down again.

He smelled a strange and sulfurous scent, which made him sneeze. Then he had a chance to look down into the narrow valley below, thick with fir, spruce, and pine, streaked with a silver line of creek at its distant bottom, from which layered drifts of mist wafted upward in veils, half hiding the great trees and drawing a line of cloud across the distant scarp that marked the ridge blocking the other end of the glen.

chapter
— 14 —

Though it had been many years since she visited the Crow Mountains, Second Son found that she remembered the steamy scent of this valley, the tang of its firs, the feel of confinement that its towering walls gave her. She was glad that this was not the place to which she intended to lead her companions for a long stay, for she would never have been content to remain here for long.

As Cleve and Kelly came down the slant toward her, she paused and pointed to the left where a shelf of protruding stone led away into the trees. No one going that way could leave a track, she knew from old wanderings here.

Only when they were well hidden beneath the huge old growth did she feel they had eluded the Absaroka who might come behind the fallen scouts and venture a short distance over the pass. Those deaths would enrage the greater band, but she hoped that not even blood vengeance would bring them into these lands that were forbidden to them.

Even those who were most enraged would not be likely to go into that valley below the ledge, she knew. Only ancient shamans and those intent upon their own deaths visited the place, her grandmother had said.

Behind her she heard the deep coughing of Holy William. She must do something about this, for not only the Crow hunted these mountains. Terrebonne, as she knew too well, had sharp ears, and she suspected that his men did, too. But there were other dangers; cougars and grizzlies inhabited the forests, and it was not good to attract their notice.

She began to glance down constantly at the growth beneath the trees, searching for the green leaves she remembered from her childhood when she followed her aunt along timbered slopes, searching for medicinal plants. But only after they passed the rocky ledge and their mounts were stepping softly on deep layers of needles and debris did she find a patch, very fresh and green in the morning sunlight.

She paused and they all dismounted, letting the horses drink from a runnel flowing out of a crack in the stone. She gathered a batch of the leaves, which grew in a pocket of damp mulch beside the little stream, and put them carefully into her pouch.

Once they stretched their cramped muscles and the horses drank their fill, she led off downward, over a mat of needles so thick and springy that tracks were almost impossible to see after a few minutes. Only the dung dropped by the animals marked their passing, and there was no way of distinguishing the droppings of an Indian pony from those of a white man's that was being fed on grass and browse.

The sun was overhead, very warm even at that altitude, and patches of snow left on the shady sides of trees and rocks were melting fast. The slopes folded about them, but Second Son watched the outthrust stones, the shapes of the trees, and before long she found what she had been searching for. Another stream dashed down over steps of rock from above them, and she turned and led Shadow and the pack animals upward again, following the brook along a crooked way that looked impossible . . . and was, unless you knew exactly where to turn and how to proceed at each angle of the route.

Yellow Hair said nothing, and the only sound from Holy William was an occasional racking cough. She noted with approval that he was trying to stifle those with his hands and a scrap of deerhide, which kept the sounds from carrying far.

Snip came lolloping up and sniffed at her hand when she reached to touch him. The notion of a dog as a companion was still strange to her, but this was such a valuable member of their group that she now thought of him as a person, another warrior with different abilities, one who could sense things that men could not.

He wagged his ropy tail and gave a soft "whuff" of greeting as he passed her and moved upward, pausing to chase a chipmunk into a cranny between two stones. He would find himself at the top of this slope very soon, she knew, for the exact course she must take was coming back to her mind sharply as she moved along from landmark to landmark.

She came up through big spruces and found herself standing on a hogback ridge. She gestured for the others to hurry, and in a few minutes they were standing beside the horses, looking down into a narrow cleft that was almost hidden beneath the mists rising from its depths. She sniffed, analyzing the scents coming to her from this fresh valley.

Pines and firs, their fragrance touched with a hint of sulfur. Plants in the midst of their brief summer blossom. The reek of a civet cat, almost thinned to nothing now, but still detectable.

Moist warmth rose from warm springs below. There was no acrid taint of wood smoke on the quiet air, and that meant that men had not come to this secret glen that her brother and her uncle had discovered so long ago.

"It is safe," she said. "This is our valley, Yellow Hair. Come down with me and see how many beaver swim the streams and how many pools their dams contain."

Wrapping his big arms about her, Cleve said, "You've done good, Second Son. I like the smell of this place, and I like the mountains all around, like walls to keep out anybody who means us harm. We'll stay here, I think, and trap and catch our breath. At least for a while."

Kelly stood silent, huddled into his deerhide shirt as if he were cold, though the summer noon was fine and the breeze only pleasantly cool. Second Son wondered again about this man, unlike anyone she knew, white or red. But she didn't speak again. Instead, she patted Cleve's arm, shrugged herself free, and set off along the path that angled down the steep slope into the spruce-dark cleft of the valley.

Even from the ridge, it was impossible to see the small river that ran along its curving bottom. Once among the trees on the slope, it was impossible to see much of anything, for the needled boughs shut away sky and sun; only the tang of sun-warmed resin surrounded them. But she knew the way.

When she had walked a route, it was forever imprinted in her memory. Second Son moved surely along the path, which perhaps was not the same game trail she had traveled in her childhood, but certainly led to the water below, as that earlier one had.

The way curved and angled, avoiding thickets of alder and small forest-fire clearings that had been taken over by brambles, fireweed, and thick-growing saplings. When she came to the drop-off that guarded the valley from casual visitors, she searched carefully along the bluff until she found the almost invisible thread of path down which they got the horses, with great difficulty.

At last they came out on the narrow verge of the stream, which was now in deep shadow because the sun had passed beyond the western barrier of cliffs, making an untimely night here at the bottom of the glen. Reflected rosiness from the eastern height above lit the ripples as the shallow creek bubbled over pebbles, and Cleve bent to drink. When he straightened, he glanced upstream and down and shook his head as he wiped his mouth on his sleeve.

"Why is this so shallow? There's still snow melting up there in the high places. It ought to be pretty full, still."

She laughed. "Yellow Hair, you have come to find the flat-tails. Upstream there are dams that hold back much of the water, unless things have changed much since I was here before. This is what escapes past the beaver dams. And the creeks that lead off from this hold small ponds that the flat-tails have made there, too. We should be able to trap in the neighboring canyons, and then here for several winters before we find their numbers dwindling."

The western walls shut out the light, shading the heights to the east, and the glen was getting darker by the moment. Second Son felt a vast relief to be here, hidden away from the French, safe, for the time, from the Absaroka.

"Come," she said, leading Shadow and her pack animals up a game track beside the water. "You will be surprised, I think, at what I will show you now."

Holy William came just behind her, riding his dun mare, for his legs were unable to walk any longer. She heard the soft thudding of the other animals' steps behind him, and beyond and above that sound she heard another noise that made her smile secretly.

"What in tarnation is that I'm hearin'?" asked Kelly. "Something's boiling up ahead, sounds like."

She didn't answer, for she was bending double to follow the trails; worn out of the undergrowth by the bodies of deer and elk and moose, they were more like tunnels than anything else. Shadow snorted irritably as branches flicked past her sensitive ears, and behind them the other animals whiffled and whinnied.

She came at last to the clearing she recalled, a small patch of grass set about with pines and spruces that formed a sort of wall on three sides, the fourth side being the stream bank itself. A heavy warmth pervaded the place, and the boiling, bubbling sound was now very near.

"We will need fire only for light," she said, loosing Shadow's reins and taking off her padding of hides that formed the saddle. There was now only a twilight under the trees and she could hardly see Cleve as he unloaded the packhorses and piled the bales of furs under a low-growing spruce.

Holy William unsaddled his mount, but he dropped to sit on the saddle, breathing hard and holding back more coughing.

Second Son saw that the animals were all tended, ready to tackle the lush grass in the meadow. "Help him," she said to Cleve. "And follow me again."

Cleve lifted the thin man effortlessly and bore him along another game trail, this one clearer, for it led among big trees that held back the underlayer of growth. She felt before her with both hands, for living things grow, and even well-remembered places change in the passing of years. But at last she came to a spot where her moccasins were warmed from beneath, and the ground was soft.

"Here." She helped Cleve set William on his feet. Once that was done, she began kindling a fire, despite the damp heat, for it was pitch-dark under the trees now, and only a drift of stars shone in the narrow slot between the ridges.

When at last a spark caught in the tinder, she sighed. Since her pregnancy, she did not have quite the energy she had known before, and now she understood why women preferred the more homebound tasks of the tribe. Carrying a child, even one as tiny as hers, took something out of her that she had not expected.

The fire blazed up along a dried pine branch, and she caught one adjacent and held it high. "Look," she said, pointing down the slant of the small rise at the cupped pool below.

Even though she had seen it before, that stone-walled pot of bubbling mud still gave her a strange feeling beneath her heart. She did not wonder that the Crow avoided such places, for it seemed that some idle god played with soil and water like a child. From time to time the bubble popped with a sound like a sigh, and that made her shiver.

"My God!" Cleve was staring down into the mud pot with amazement. "Can you cook in it? Is it hot enough?"

"Not here. Just above, where the hot spring runs out of the hill. But this should help William's cough, don't you think?"

William had the same thought. Without taking off his hat, he stripped off his worn leathers and the long underwear they had given him from Henri's stores, as well as his moccasins, and waded out into the hot mud, his skin, stretched tightly over his racklike ribs, blue and goose-pimpled. But the warmth was already helping, for a rosy flush rose up his back, and his knobby rump began to glow scarlet.

Second Son laughed. "Bury yourself well in the mud, William," she said. "Soak in it while we cook. There is a hot pool to wash in when you are done here."

Somehow, the spot they chose for a permanent camp seemed remote and very safe, though the cries of hunting wolves sounded from the heights above and the occasional irritable grunt of a grizzly echoed down the valley. Their first camp they made against a rock wall where the steaming spring bubbled out of the cliff. Their fire provided light, but the hot spring heated the area so well that Second Son suspected even winter would not freeze the space surrounding the bubbling pool and the runnel that filled it.

After their first evening there, when they slept with

feet to the fire and kept watch turn by turn, she suggested that they erect a tipi to keep their equipment dry. Rain was frequent in summer, sometimes mixed with snow, and if they were to live comfortably, they needed shelter.

With Cleve, she climbed the sloping sides of the glen, below the drop-off, and cut lodgepoles. They hid the raw stumps with dried leaves and needles, smoothing the disturbed needle mat until only one who smelled with the senses of an animal would know that men had been there. The fragrant branches they carried back to camp for bedding. It was not Second Son's way to leave sign that she had passed or to waste anything.

Once the tipi was erected, the area beside the cliff seemed friendlier at once. William, soaked daily in his mud bath, coughed less and less and finally stopped altogether. His skinny frame began putting on weight, for Cleve and Snip went out often and brought back woodchucks or rabbits or grouse for the pot, and even the preacher's snaggled teeth were able to manage the thick stews Cleve made.

They did not begin trapping, of course, for in summer the beaver shed and their fur became unsalable. Instead, they ranged up and down the glen, over into the next, where they found numerous dams and lodges, and even back into the steamy valley they had first seen, searching for creeks with active colonies.

Cleve drew on a deerhide a rough map of the area they scouted and taught her to read the sooty markings he made. Since her people often marked crude maps into dust or mud, she learned quickly and soon could indicate her own discoveries accurately. Before fall was well under way, their plans were made, the traps taken from Henri's cabin were ready for use, and all were filled with anticipation for the winter's work.

In those months, Second Son found her steps growing slower, her body thickening, her balance shifting. She worked hard to overcome those inconveniences, but her energies were even less than before, though her strength was always a part of her and did not lessen. As the days shortened and the sun's brief excursion into the glen lost intensity, she went out early each morning and ran along the creek, measuring her strides, keeping her breath even and her pace rapid. Allowing her body to betray her into weakness was not a thing she would endure.

So early, the beaver were usually just beginning to surface after swimming out of their lodges, their eyes gleaming in the light reflected off the water, their coats sleek with wet. Sometimes they slapped their tails against the water on seeing her. She always passed dams, noting how old ones were repaired with fresh saplings and logs after the worst of the runoff had done its damage.

About the ponds, the alders and birches were cut back to a distance by the busy teeth of the animals, and there she picked up her pace. For seasons to come they would not trouble the beaver on those ponds, saving them for a source of fur if other areas ran short.

Even as she trotted along, Second Son was mentally placing traps along the creeks that meandered from the cliffs to find the stream. She had acquired a taste for trapping in her brief time with Henri and Cleve along the Belle Fourche. This was a thing that her people did only as children, snaring rabbits and other rodents for the pot. Doing it as a grown-up was somehow pleasant to her.

Her running worried Cleve, who had a number of strange white man's notions about childbearing. Often Second Son wondered what sort of weaklings the women of the white race must be if they made such a difficulty of producing a new life. She had seen her own aunt squat on the grassland, allowing the rest of the band to proceed on its way while she gave birth to an infant, which she wiped off, wrapped in a soft skin, and laid in the grass while she tended to herself and buried the afterbirth. Once Second Son had carried a newly acquired kinsman as she ran with Strutting Bird after the dwindling shapes of the Burning Hearts.

She found herself thinking about such matters as she moved through the fall days, working with the men to set up a shelter sufficient to keep Holy William from freezing, for he flatly refused to share their tipi. His reason for that escaped her until he spelled it out plainly.

"The worst things that ever happened to me in all my life, they taken place in a tipi. I'd rather sleep in a blizzard with my back to a bear than go inside one ever again." His face, not so thin now, was set in stubborn lines, and Second Son saw, behind the weathered tan and the map of lines, a glimpse of the pain the preacher hid within.

Cleve, who sat beside her at the evening fire, put his arm about her and squeezed her shoulders. She felt in him that strange sensitivity that none of her own menfolk showed, if, indeed, they possessed it at all.

Again she marveled that one who had escaped the Arikara, killing his pursuer with his hands, survived to find her people, and battled Piegan to the last warrior could show his feelings without shame. And yet she liked this in him, and she did not hide that liking.

"We'll build you a fine shanty, William," he said, and she nodded in agreement. A home was important; she understood that as only a nomad could.

Their own quarters were now snug, ready to repel snow or rain or wind with its efficient conical shape, which held the warmth down instead of letting it rise into corners. But if Holy William wanted his own house, Second Son was willing to help build it.

Time dragged now, for they had accumulated enough dried meat, herbs, and seeds to see them through the winter. They had begun to set traps in the next valley, as the weather turned, but they had not yet placed the most of them along the creeks feeding into its larger stream. Running those they had out took little time, even with the difficult climb into and out of the steep glen, and Cleve or William could do it in a few hours.

So she helped with the shanty, watching with some scorn the building methods the white men used. Many poles were wasted to raise walls that could not be taken down and moved but must stand there to rot, once William left the valley. But the poles, when chinked with mud from the mud pot, held out the wind, and the layered spruce boughs of the roof kept out most of the rain and should hold out the coming snow.

Smoke escaped through a hole in the roof, and through that raindrops could fall straight into the fire. In a properly regulated tipi the smoke hole was not a problem. As well, the flaps could be moved to accommodate a shifting wind, making it draw out fumes from the fire. White men did many things in an inefficient and wasteful way, she was learning, and it puzzled her.

But the shanty was finished quickly, with three sets of strong hands and three willing backs devoted to its construction. Flat stones from the creek bed formed the fireplace in one corner of the square room, and on the night when William moved from his sleeping spot beneath the drooping branches of a spruce, he held a feast at his own hearth.

It was almost winter, and the growing chill assured them that any furs would be thick and glossy. Leaves had fallen from alder and birch, and the waters of the creek and ponds beyond the reach of the hot spring were growing very cold. In their trapping valley, it was time to begin their endeavors in earnest.

The wind was sweeping over the northwestern ridge, eddying in the glen, bringing with it a spit of sleet. As Second Son made her way from her tipi to the shanty, she could see steam rising thick from the mud pot and the hot spring. Winter had come early this year.

Cleve bent and entered William's house, and she followed, feeling the cold wind at her back as she let the doorhide drop and tied it down with thongs. Kelly had a bright fire sputtering in the hearth, in the inefficient white man's way of burning crossed sticks at their middles. But his pot was simmering, and he had a pair of grouse on a spit, dripping their fat into the coals.

He seemed genuinely happy, and for the first time Second Son warmed to him. He was not like anyone she knew, but she now understood that there were many things she didn't know, had never seen, and could not understand. There was no harm in Holy William, she was now certain, and she sat beside Cleve and toasted her moccasined feet before the fire.

The mud-chinked walls did not keep out the worst gusts, and she knew, as they ate and talked, that it was getting colder outside. When at last she untied the thongs and opened the flap, snowflakes prickled her face.

She turned back and said, "Here is the snow. The beaver should be in prime condition now, and it is time to put out all our traps. Tomorrow, Yellow Hair?"

He looked past her, nodded briskly, and stepped out into the cloud of fat flakes. "Tomorrow. We'll be on our way by dawn. Sleep tight, Kelly, if you want to keep up with us."

Together they moved along the path, which was warmed by the nearby hot spring and was melting the snow as it fell. Their tipi loomed ahead, the coals left smoldering inside glowing faintly through the tough hide wall.

Second Son felt a surge of warmth fill her. Tomorrow the trapping would begin in earnest. And in a few more moons there would be a child in their house. What a fine life she had gained when she took this warrior captive!

chapter
— 15 —

When snow began to fly, it became obvious to Jules that it was going to be a severe winter, though that was nothing unusual in the mountain country. Instead of making his base camp in the Bighorns, he had moved on into the Absarokas, and now his men were strung out along three creeks that the beaver had turned into a complex of ponds in the basin he had discovered.

Each cabin held three or four trappers. More men crowded together, he'd found years ago, made trouble when cooped up for long periods by the weather. He shared his own shanty with no one, which caused some grumbling among his trappers.

"Think you're too good to sit cheek by jowl with Americans?" asked Ben Yoder, one of the few Yankees he had admitted to his group.

He wanted to hit the man, but he gritted his teeth and tried to smile. "I am getting old, me," he said. "Sometime the bone he hurt, and the mind he run like rabbit. If one snore at night, I do not sleep, and that make me ver' angry. So it is better if I sleep alone. The house, she is small, not like yours. I do the thinking for us all, *mon ami*, and for that I must have the rest."

The others looked skeptical, though Philippe, who had known him longest of all, grinned. But it was true that the hut he built would have been uncomfortable for two, and they said little more. Teasing their leader had proven to be a dangerous pastime, Terrebonne knew, for he had deliberately concentrated on making it so.

Beaver were plentiful in the basin he had chosen, though grizzlies were thick on the ground as well, and they had to keep a constant lookout for Crow. Marten, mink, wolverine, and other small game abounded. Running the traps was a matter of keeping one eye on the surrounding country and one hand on your weapon, which made taking up traps and removing the limp shapes of beaver a much more difficult task.

Luckily, there proved to be no Crow nearby, and he was grateful for that. They were always a danger here in these dark mountains, for he had crossed wills with one of their chiefs, years ago. But this winter they had evidently set up their cold-weather villages in remote valleys too distant to bring their hunters near his home base.

Plews were strung high on the walls of shanties,

hung on their willow frames, and Terrebonne counted them with much satisfaction every time he patrolled the area. Those fools who spent their days tramping in the snow, freezing their hands on the steel of the traps and the dead animals, would take their share, it was true, to a trading fort or to a rendezvous for trading, which the Yankee fur trader Ashworth was arranging.

They would get fresh powder, lead for their rifle balls, whiskey to make them forget the endless winter days when there was nothing to do but quarrel or fight among themselves. They would buy women . . . He gritted his teeth for the thousandth time, thinking of what that Cheyenne bitch had done to him when he attacked her.

But that meant he would retain far more of his payment than any of these *canaille*. He did not drink whiskey—not much, at any rate. He would get what supplies he needed, but he would, this year, have no need for baubles for a squaw or pay for her husband or father for the use of her. His hoard of gold coins, hidden safely in a very secret place, would grow this year, and perhaps one day he would return to France, rich beyond the dreams of his peasant brothers.

The thought pleased him as he walked the path to the network of ponds where he had set his own traps. He would take passage in a cabin rather than crossing in the hold as he had done before on his way to New Orleans. He would be dressed in fine clothing of wool and broadcloth and wear a tall beaver hat as a symbol of the source of his wealth. A diamond the size of his thumbnail would adorn his left hand.

He glanced down at that, frowning at the missing middle finger. The wrappings in which he swaddled his palm and fingers when he went out into the cold did not hide that loss, and again he cursed the long-dead nobleman who had his manservant amputate it when he caught the child Jules stealing fruit from his orchards.

The breath came harshly between his teeth as the Frenchman stepped over a downed tree and moved toward the first trap, his moccasins crunching in the half-frozen damp of the soil. That had been the day when he declared his secret war upon the world, though no one else had known that for a very long while.

Maman had wept when the Comte de Brassis's man dragged her son home by his neck, as if he were a disobedient puppy. The master was at his heels.

"Control your spawn, woman," the lord had spat at her, "or the next time I find him trespassing upon my lands I shall remove his head."

That was no idle threat, and both mother and son knew it. The master had the power of life and death over his people, still, for the great Revolution was yet in the future. Even after forty years, Jules still felt the shudder of dread that had shaken him then.

But he had taken his revenge when the people rose at last against their oppressors. He had nailed the infant son of Renaud LeFevre, Comte de Brassis, to the great wooden doors of his house, and he had stuck beside it the head of the father, slamming it down upon a spike driven into the carved cross that guarded that portal.

He liked to think that the expression of terror the dead face still held was directed toward him, which it easily could have been. Jules had been in the forefront of the group that caught the fleeing horse before it could pass the confines of the De Brassis lands and secured its desperate rider, who was holding his son in his arm.

He had cut the throat of the horse himself, and then he helped drag the count from his saddle, wrenching the nobleman's trapped leg from beneath his fallen mount. How the man had screamed when they castrated him—Jules wondered suddenly if some sort of divine retribution had overtaken him for wielding that knife, so many years ago. He shook away the thought.

They had made the comte watch while the child was strangled and nailed to the door, beyond which the screams of his mother and her maids, being enthusiastically raped by former chattels, sounded shrilly. By the time they beheaded him, Renaud LeFevre seemed not to care at all.

Jules's younger brothers had hidden in the hills afterward, but he had gone out of the *vallée* de Brassis to join the army when the great Napoleon rose up to make France great again. He almost felt pride at being a part, though a small and inept one, of that great army. When the word came that the Emperor of France had retired in defeat, Jules had almost wept.

He kicked aside the brush with which he had hidden his trail to the water and knelt to tug at the line holding his trap. The device caught the beaver as he swam beneath the water after leaving its lodge, and the creature drowned. That was a safety measure, for those teeth that chewed down trees as thick as his waist or thicker were quite capable of amputating still another finger from the hand of Jules Terrebonne.

He pulled the sodden shape onto shore and took it out of the trap, admiring the quality of the pelt. Even dead, that was an admirable creature, almost four feet in length, its fur streaked with water but, beneath the top layer, still dry and almost warm. It would bring a good price.

Terrebonne gutted and skinned the animal and hung it in a tree, for when he had his catch for the morning he would take it back to his house. Beaver tail, roasted over the fire, was a delicacy.

Rising to his feet, he stared out over the pond, which was large enough to contain a half-dozen lodges. There was trapping here to keep him busy for several seasons, he knew, if he could keep his men together and control them.

But thoughts of France had intruded on his solitary morning, and not one of his men, even Philippe, ventured to interrupt his routine. Tramping through the light layer of snow left by the last flurry, Terrebonne saw behind his eyes the face of his mother when he left the valley. She had wept, not at losing this son who had been only a grief to her but at the permanent change in her life his going meant.

He laughed bitterly. Of the Terrebonnes left in the *vallée* de Brassis, which of his brothers cared for the old woman? Or was she dead now, lying with his father beneath the crooked wooden marker in a corner of the graveyard beneath the shadow of the village church?

Thinking of the church, of Père Villefois, of his many beatings at the hands of the priest and the torments that followed them, he found himself sweating, even in the cold. There was no one who would protect the child of a peasant from the abuses of a priest. Who would believe, if he had said to them, "The *père* has done thus and so to me"?

Only when he had helped to pull down the church and hang its priest did he learn that many owners of the willing hands helping him had suffered the same cruelty. Which might explain why few young peasants of the village ever could be said to become religious.

"God will punish you!" his mother had cried, when she learned of the sacrilege.

"His priest has already done that," Jules told her, and he proceeded to describe to the horrified woman exactly how her trusted cleric had tortured him and the other small boys in his parish.

He had left her distraught, in tears for the loss of the one thing that had given her poor life meaning. At times he almost regretted this, but then he would recall the face of Père Villefois as he was stood upon a bench in the cemetery of his own church and called to account by those he had abused. When the noose went about his neck, he had shrieked, but was cut off in midcry, as the bench was jerked away.

Jules grimaced, half grin, half frown, as he saw again the lanky legs kicking reflexively, the stain of urine spreading down the exposed stocking and dripping from one black slipper. He had slipped back, after all was quiet that night, and beaten the still, dark shape with a stick, making it swing erratically at the end of the rope, and the branch from which it hung creak dolefully.

Had God indeed punished him for that terrible deed? Jules snorted and moved toward his next trap. If so, it was worth the price. He had torn from his heart the smolder of hatred for nobles and churchmen and let it burn itself clean. Now he was merely a thief and a murderer of the ordinary sort, although he had found a new and fresher world in which to conduct his business.

Jules stumbled and almost fell. That made him watch his footing more closely. He neared the little inlet where a trove of stored birch, alder, and willow branches was stored in the water for winter use by the beaver and moved toward the track where the animal came out of the water to reach his larder. Curled into a huddle against the stack was a shape that was not any four-footed animal.

A man lay there, blue with cold though he was wrapped in a tattered bit of deerhide, unconscious but not, Jules thought, quite dead. A spy from some other who had seen the opportunity offered by isolated groups of trappers?

He turned the body over, staring into the face. Brown eyes opened and looked blindly up at him. The mouth opened, too, but no words came out.

Merde! Terrebonne stooped over the half-dead man and hauled him up, laying him over one burly shoulder. He could have let him freeze without qualm, but he would not be satisfied until he knew that this was not a scout for some group posing a threat to his own operation.

Halfway back to the camp he met Ben, who had stayed behind to hang the hides skinned out the day before. "A visitor, he have come to our camp," Terrebonne said, dumping the deadweight into the Yankee's arms. "Come with me. We mus' learn who he is and why he may be here. We want no competition for this spot, *n'est-ce pas?*"

"Looks like he'll die before you can learn much," Yoder said. "But I'll put him in my shanty. Yours is too small to swing a cat. Then we'll find out what we can. He's dressed like an Injun, but lots of us are. He might be white under all that dirt."

"I will go back and bring in my beaver. Then we will see," Terrebonne said. "You build up your fire, *oui?* I shall return at once to help you revive this man and learn what he know."

That proved to be a long process. The boy, for so he proved to be once they peeled off the filthy bit of robe he had wrapped about him and the even filthier deerhide shirt beneath it, was very young and terribly thin.

His body was Indian dark, they found. Scars were netted across his back and buttocks, newer ones crisscrossing old ones, and his hands were broken, his face bruised.

"He have been a slave," said Terrebonne. "And not of a kind master. I can assure you that he will not ever forget what have been done to him. He will be wild and angry, not to be trust, no matter what we do for him or to him."

Yoder stared at him over the small fire centering the shanty. After examining the boy, he had covered him with a robe and retreated to his own bed pile, where he sat waiting for some decision from his leader.

"You know that for a fact, do you?" he asked, his tone wry. "Know all about that from personal experience?"

Terrebonne stared back, surprised at this accurate guess on the part of one he had suspected of being dull-witted. He was in the habit of discounting Americans automatically as upstart *canaille*, but this one seemed to know more than appeared on the surface.

"That is as may be," he said. "Watch him close, *mon ami*. If he revive, come after me. I would question him myself."

But as he stalked away again toward his traps he thought of that thin young face, battered and cut, and felt those wounds upon his own long-ago features. He knew, indeed, what happened with that one, for he was himself the product of such treatment. Whatever he did could be laid at the doors of those who had tortured him as a child.

Then, with the strength of will that had carried him so far from his roots, he put the newcomer out of his mind and finished running his traps. His take was good, yet it was not so good as he had expected in this rich trapping ground. Thinking over the take so far this fall and winter, he began to believe that he had not, after all, discovered the best place in the Absarokas to set up his new base camp.

With that in mind, he returned to his shanty in darkness, amid a flurry of snow. The communal kettle was simmering over an outdoor fire, and his companions had gathered about it, putting into the pot what tidbits they had gathered and spitting over the shimmering coals choice cuts of venison or beaver tail or bear paw.

"You want me to take that fellow somethin' to eat?" Yoder asked him as he stalked to his usual position and sank onto his heels in the warmth.

"You feed him, he will vomit when I question him," Jules said. "I like those I talk with to be ver' weak, empty, without resistance, *comprends*?"

Yoder nodded, his eyes bright. Terrebonne had noticed that he enjoyed slitting the throats of beasts, killing from ambush, entertaining the group with tales of his stay with the Lakota before he joined this group. Some of the descriptions of torture were colorful, though Terrebonne thought privately that they might well be touched with more imagination than fact. Now, seeing the avid expression on Yoder's weathered face, he wondered if those lurid accounts might not be true.

He ate in silence, thinking of the things he wanted to extract from the boy inside the Yoder shanty. It was best to do this sort of thing correctly and in logical order, in case the victim died before divulging all you desired to learn. With the very young, very frail-looking person involved this time, it might even be best to begin with kindness.

When the last trapper had belched deeply, picked his teeth with the tip of a skinning knife, and ambled off to his own quarters, it left Philippe, Yoder, Sanchez, and Terrebonne to linger over the fire that burned between their two shelters. Neither Yoder nor his leader had mentioned the captive hidden inside, and now it was time to deal with this problem, without the distraction of other advice or suggestions. The boys would be delighted at such unexpected entertainment, but that wasn't what was needed at this point.

Yoder went into his hide-flapped door hole and came out holding the youth as if he were a child. He dropped him onto the ground beside the fire, jarring a grunt of pain from the young man, and the robe fell open, revealing the scars and the frostbitten skin of his hands and arms.

Terrebonne knelt beside the thin shape and stared into the brown eyes. *"Français?"* he asked, though he had no hope of that.

There was no comprehension in the gaze that met his. He turned and spat into the fire. When he looked down again, he said, "Absaroka? Lakota? Tsistsistas?"

Through the grime and rawness of the face, the jaw muscles tensed as if the boy had gritted his teeth. "I am . . . Darnell," he said in English. "Not . . . Indian."

"Who have done this to you?" the Frenchman asked, interested. That was no American twist to those English words.

"Pawnee," he said. There was little breath behind the word, and his eyes closed as if uttering it had taken the last of his energy.

"Are you spy for someone? Other trapper, perhaps?" Jules kept his tone soft and friendly. He reached for a tin cup and gestured for Yoder to put some of the remaining broth from the stew into it. This one must have strength to speak, though it was a waste of good food.

The eyes opened again as if even that were a terrible effort. They had lost focus, and Terrebonne knew he had not understood the question. He took the cup of broth, blew on it to cool it, for a scalded tongue does not speak readily, and held it to the boy's lips.

"You drink this. It will help you to be strong, yes? And then you may tell us what we mus' know."

The knobby throat bobbled as the liquid went down in gulps. For a moment the thin face seemed warmed, but then the body tensed, spasmed, and he rolled onto his side and vomited. It had been a long while, Jules thought, since he ate last.

Again Terrebonne cooled a bit of broth, this time thinning it with snow. "You drink ver' slow, eh? That help you to keep it down, perhaps."

Darnell sipped carefully. His thin face tightened with pain as he tried to wrap his hands about the cup, and Terrebonne saw that the nails had been ripped from several fingers. That, with returning circulation to the parts around the frozen areas, would account for a lot, he thought.

Philippe stared at him over the boy's head, his brows quirked quizzically. "So we are to do this thing in a civilized way, eh?" his gaze asked.

Jules nodded briefly, and his lieutenant rose and

went into the cabin. In a moment he came out again clutching a bottle. It was the diluted rotgut the trader at the fort pawned off on his desperate trapper customers, but in the present condition of this captive, any alcohol at all should loosen his tongue nicely. Torture was amusing, but it wasted time if quicker means could be found.

"Ici, mon ami," he said, taking the bottle and tipping some of its muddy contents into the cup. "This will warm you."

Again the young man sipped. He didn't choke, as one would have thought, when the fiery contents went down his throat. Instead his face took on a bit of color, and his eyes brightened. When he returned the cup to Terrebonne, it was empty.

"Now," said Jules, "you tell us who you are, why you are here, *non?* We are honest men, trappers of the *vair*, but we have many enemy, and we mus' be cautious, you see."

Darnell tried weakly to push himself up, but moaned and sank back when he attempted to put any weight on his abused hands. Philippe, looking even more quizzical, thrust a roll of beaver hides under his head, and the boy sighed.

"Yes, I can see that," he murmured. "I learned too late that one must protect himself against the unexpected villain." He was growing pale again, and Terrebonne passed him another slug of rotgut. Again he sipped it, and the liquor revived him.

"Where you from?" grunted Yoder. "You don't sound like nobody from my part of the world. English?"

"Yes. I came over from London with Lord Cholmondeley. I was his nephew and he made me his amanuensis."

Yoder looked aghast. "His own nephew? My God, what sort of men are these Englishmen, anyway?"

Darnell laughed, painfully and unexpectedly, until he choked again and Terrebonne pounded his back. When he had regained his breath, he said, "I am sorry. I was his *secretary.* That is all. I wrote his letters, took care that things got into the post, when there was a post into which to get them, and dressed down his valet when the man was too drunk to assist His Lordship."

"Then howinell did you get way out here?" Yoder persisted.

Terrebonne, who wondered the same thing, sat back and let the American do the questioning. He seemed to be getting through nicely, and now the young man was obviously feeling comfortable with him. This was going to be easier than he had expected.

"There was a hunter who came to New Orleans boasting about the great bears, the tremendous buffalo, the elk and moose to be found here in these wide plains. When His Lordship completed his mission, he decided that he must travel into those wonderful hunting lands with this Nimrod, who was called Pierre Mouton. Nothing would dissuade him.

"Of course, he must have his secretary and his valet, his tent and his cook and his conveniences with him, for nothing less would be suitable for one in his station. So we packed up enough goods to supply a voyage across the ocean and we set out up the Mississippi, up the Missouri, and across country once we came to the river for which Mouton headed."

Again Darnell's voice wavered and his eyes dimmed, and again his cup was replenished. The liquor went down in a gulp this time. Terrebonne could almost see the alcohol burning inside the pale body, and he wondered what it might be doing to the insides of this interesting young man. Not that it mattered.

"So how did you come to be in the hands of the Pawnee?" That was Ben again, his dogged mind obviously wrestling hard to digest all this information.

Darnell moved his shoulders restlessly, and Ben pushed the hard bundle of furs further beneath his head and back.

"We had horses with us, moving along the embankment, though we traveled on a keelboat. When we reached the Indian village that Mouton intended as our jumping-off place, we disembarked and began our journey. We traveled for weeks, and even after we could see the mountains on the horizon, it required many days to reach them."

"Get to the point," Yoder said. He kicked the end of a log into the fire and took a gulp of his own from Philippe's bottle.

The boy nodded, closing his eyes. "I went to relieve myself beyond a growth of bushes. While I was squatting there, I heard a terrible scream and then shots. By the time I got back to the camp, it was a scene to rival anything in hell.

"His Lordship was lying, covered with blood, across the chair where he sat every evening; his tent was in flames. The cook was being scalped, and the valet was not to be seen.

"Mouton"—the young voice was very bitter now— "was counting out the contents of the satchel in which we carried the funds for the trip while the savages took what they wanted, scattered the rest, and took turns stabbing the four men whom Mouton had hired as horse handlers and guards."

"So that was when the Pawnee taken you," Yoder said. "How long was you in their hands, younker?"

"But that was not the Pawnee. Not then. I have no idea who they were, for I could speak no Indian dialect and knew nothing of their ways. They were not kind, but as I learned later, they were not cruel. At least, not by their own lights.

"I was a slave there for months, but they treated me no worse than the other slaves they had captured. Then they, too, were raided, and the Pawnee dragged me away, along with the women and two children of the one who called himself my master."

Terrebonne leaned forward and dolloped more liquor into the tin cup. The boy's tongue was growing a bit thick, though he still spoke readily, with that clipped accent making his words plain.

"They were beasts. They dragged me behind their horses until I was scraped and cut almost to the bone. When they reached their camp, they tied me to a post and laid burning brands againsh—against my back and my ribs. It was weeks before I was able to walk, and I will nev' know why they din' . . . didn't kill me."

"But did you see any white men there at that time? Or later?" Jules could contain his questions no longer, and he again leaned forward to stare into those pale eyes.

"Yesh. Yes. I saw a pair of white men . . . riding with a warrior. Packhorsh . . . horses carrying bales of furs. That was . . . how long? . . . Weeksh, now. I wanted to run to them, to make them take me along, but then I wondered if those were like that bastard Mouton. Thought they shaw . . . saw me. Hid again and didn't come out. Would they turn me over to the

Pawnee again and go their way? I had enough. Enough . . ." His voice trailed off.

"Where? Where did you see those two?" Terrebonne had a gut feeling that they might well be the enigmatic warrior he had seen on the tower by the Belle Fourche and the man who had escaped the Piegan.

If it were they, who was the other man? But that could be learned later. More whites now wandered the mountains than he cared to think about. The country was filling up, and it was no longer the wild, free place he had known in his youth.

"Somewhere 'tween this range and that other'n to th' east," muttered Darnell.

"Tell me where!" insisted the trapper.

"Little river. Rock looks like a crouching man. I hid—hic!—behin' that and watched them go. They went up cut, into mountains. This range? Think sho . . ." And the voice stopped at last.

Jules rose to his feet, feeling a vast satisfaction rise within him. The bales must contain Henri Lavallette's fur harvest for the past three years. Whether or not these were the ones he had been seeking, it would be well worth his time to scout them out, for taking those plews would be not only a pleasure but a duty.

He nudged the limp body with the toe of a moccasin. There was no response.

"Cut his throat," he said to Philippe, and turned away to his own cabin and his plans for the next spring.

chapter
— 16 —

William Kelly was proving to be more help than Cleve had expected when he decided to bring him along. Once the preacher had satisfied himself that the trapper and the warrior were solidly married according to his own personal beliefs, he turned a blind eye to any canoodling they might do. Not that there was much now.

Cleve sighed and loosed the willow frame, which sprang into shape, stretching a beaver pelt taut. As he began another he watched Second Son, though he pretended not to. She didn't like her present condition. If she had actually been a man and a warrior, she could not have been more appalled at the changes in her tough, young body.

She was, he decided, shaped like a pear, her strong shoulders dwarfed by the expanse of her distended stomach. Always sparing of her affections, which, she explained patiently to him, was the way in which her people limited their population, she was now toucheous. Mighty toucheous, in fact.

She slept little, for Little Whatsit, as he privately called the child in her belly, kicked ferociously when she lay down. Indeed, he had given up sleeping too close to his wife, for the youngster had been known to kick his father through his mother's intervening flesh. He'd never have believed an unborn baby could kick so damn hard!

He had felt abused for a while, when Second Son seemed not to want him to touch her, even for a pat or a hug, but once Cleve sat down and thought it out, he understood that she had to be so uncomfortable that she wanted to shout and scream and lash out at somebody. Not that she ever did, of course. That iron control from her Cheyenne heritage never let her do anything so unmanly.

Except get pregnant . . . but he kept that as a private joke. She wouldn't, he felt certain, appreciate that one. Not at the moment, if ever.

Meanwhile, they all worked industriously. Kelly had located a high cave, sloughed out of the rock of one of the cliffs forming a wall of the valley, and there they had stored their bales, safe from damp and wind. No bear could den there, for it was a hole in the cliff so high that they had to let down a rope from above, tie on the bales, and haul them up, using Socks as power.

They'd had to make a lot more line for that, but it was worth it to have the plews safe above flood level, out of reach of random animals. Even chipmunks and mice found nothing in the bare rock, so far from food and water, to attract them, and Cleve hoped to have the bales safely removed before spring might set them wandering, revealing this new source of nibbling material.

The trapping had been good, though they had not set their snares in their own canyon. The dams there were, by necessity, small ones, and the ponds were limited, but each held at least two or three lodges, and those seemed to be filled with great numbers of beaver. These were saved for later, for Cleve and Second Son felt that this would be a safe haven and a sure source of plews for years to come, if they harvested the area carefully.

So he and Kelly climbed the perilous track Cleve had found zigzagging up one of the cliffs beyond the creek, making their way every morning over the rim of their hidden valley into a wider one beyond. That was dotted with ponds and laced with meandering streams having their sources in springs descending from the mountain on its western edge. It was so difficult of access that there was no sign that even the Crow visited it.

Second Son was now so heavy and out of balance that she seldom risked the climb, remaining behind to dress skins or to do chores about the tipi and Kelly's rough shanty. However, this morning was the first clear and sunny one in days, the air chill and clean enough to scour out your lungs. As Cleve readied his pack to leave she joined him.

"Today I shall go with you, Yellow Hair. It may be the last time I am able, and I must stretch my muscles and leave this narrow space. The wide plains are my home, giving a clear view from sky to sky, and I feel trapped behind these stone walls." In preparation for the climb, she had braided her hair tightly and tied it with thongs; her feet were shod in double moccasins, the outer layer having hair left on the surface of the sole for traction on slippery patches.

Cleve had learned that trying to coddle a Cheyenne warrior was not a thing to be undertaken lightly. Kelly, however, grunted. "You sure?" he asked her. "You look like a walking tipi. Don't seem safe to me."

The glance from her black eyes could have cut him off at the knees, if he'd caught it. Cleve saw and said, "Oh, William, she'll be all right. You go first and I'll come behind, and if she falls off the mountain, she'll take me with her."

Kelly snorted, but he started off toward the track leading to the crossing, where they had felled a log across the narrowest part of the creek below a dam. There in the deep slot between mountains, warmed by the hot springs, the air usually remained warm enough to melt most of the snow; the beaver ponds had never entirely frozen over.

They walked, silent-footed, over needle-furred ground, softened by snows, until they came to the lip of stone that hid the ascending route.

Only lungs accustomed to long months in the high country could sustain that climb. Muscles hardened to the work creaked and ears popped as they went upward. It grew colder, the higher they went, and before they reached the top Cleve looked back at their valley, to see a drift of steam hiding the treetops below.

Beneath his moccasins the trail grew icy. When they emerged from the canyon into the great firs and spruces above, they found, as usual, the high forest covered with snow, deep and drifted. The billows were now dirty with fallen leaves and needles, yellowed and stained.

In days the thaw would begin, though Second Son said that even in midsummer there would still be traces of snow in pockets protected from the sun. Now it seemed the depths of winter rather than the last few weeks before spring.

Cleve forged ahead, once they were on more level ground, and sought out the route he always took into that other valley. The morning, which had begun as bright and cold, was clouding over by the time they were down the ridge and once more in low ground, where hot springs and bubbling mud warmed the air just above the freezing point. Each of the three took a section of the trapping streams and ponds and set to work.

The traps had been set near the spots where beaver had cut branches of poplar, alder, and birch and thrust them deep into the mud of the pond bottom. The tops, now bare with skinny fingers trailing above the surface, revealed those food stores plainly, and it was easy to pick out good spots to place the snares.

The traps were not all filled, but the catch was a good one, and as Cleve took up his he rubbed them with castoreum from glands in the fresh-caught animals. That hid the human scent and would not frighten away another member of the beaver family. Trapping was almost over for the season, but he automatically treated the traps before stacking them for retrieving later.

This larger canyon would be years in the trapping, he felt certain. Now that they had dressed out the plews caught before the iron freezes set in, there would be all they could carry out with them, for they would leave in a few weeks now.

Beyond the shoulder of the mountain to the west was still another long valley where many large lodges were visible, even from so far. Without changing base camps, they should be able to take furs for a long time to come. For now they had just about enough.

He had no intention of leaving stashes of bales to be found by intruders. No, they would set out when the passes cleared, taking with them a goodly sum in beaver. When they returned, they would have fresh supplies of everything they needed.

And the baby? As Second Son told him, it would come when it came, and nobody would worry until that time arrived.

He had learned the hard way to keep his ears open, his eyes sweeping the landscape about him even while his hands were busy. That was why, when a bulky shape, swaddled in rank-smelling furs, came volleying out of the willows, he was able to pivot on his heel, letting the full force of that assault unbalance him without smashing him flat.

Before he hit the ground he was yelling "Kelly!" as loudly as he could. Then his hands were filled with the attacker's right wrist, holding it desperately. Inching toward his chest was a blade wielded by an arm so much stronger than his own that he thought instantly of his father. That was the sort of iron strength forged by years of hard work and constant effort.

The face glaring down into his was bearded, dark, and savage. Only the light eyes told him he had been attacked by a white man. That didn't make his struggle any easier, for the body on top of his was like a slab of stone, hard and heavy and immovable.

Cleve dug in his heels and arched his back with all his strength, heaving against the bulk on top of him. The man's weight shifted just enough to allow Cleve to begin to roll.

Instantly, those steely arms were holding him again,

but now the younger man had gained purchase, and he managed to get both hands set enough to twist the knife hand and force the blade out, sending it splashing into the mud beside the pond.

His knees came up as the other lunged after the weapon. When they sank into the midsection of the fur-clad stranger, he went over backward with a splash into the half-frozen mud of the edge of the pond.

Cleve rolled away and onto his feet in one motion, reaching for his own knife. As his fingers closed on the haft a pair of huge arms wrapped around him from behind. Heart lurching against his ribs, Cleve kicked backward, jerked his head back to break the nose of the man holding him.

But this one was an old hand at dirty fighting, he discovered. The nose wasn't there, and the knees slid away without damage from the jabs of his heels. With one heave, the attacker lifted Cleve off his feet, all two hundred pounds of him clearing the ground as easily as if he were a baby.

The other man was coming now, a smile curling his straggling black mustache upward. Again he held the knife, and this time there was no way to escape.

Now Cleve hoped that neither Kelly nor Second Son had heard his call. They should hide until these villains finished their dirty work and left, for Second Son was not in any shape for a fight, and William hadn't regained his strength. Cleve had a good idea what this bastard wanted, and he had no intention of telling him where Henri's furs were hidden. That store would give his child a start in the world, if his mother and Kelly managed well.

"So. You, I think, may be the one I have look for so long," said his first attacker. "But for you, I would find the beaver that Lavallette store for two winter, back on the Belle Fourche. I go to harvest my careful crop, and all is *fini*. No cabin, no Henri, and no fur. You have steal them, *cochon*, and I want them. I find the skull of my watcher there, and you owe me a life also."

Cleve managed to control his start of recognition. He had never seen the man, but he knew there was only one this might be. "Lavallette told me about a thief and murderer who preyed on his fellow trappers. Henri killed one watcher on the Bad Gods' Tower, and he was sure the man was your spy. Oh, I've heard a *lot* about you."

"Henri, he always have talk too much, *n'est-ce pas*? But I think you have take care of that well. You talk of thief—you have take the store of *vair* that Lavallette have collected for three winter. What do you call that, eh?" The pale eyes glittered with a light that gave Cleve a cold feeling in his bones.

"The spoils of war," he said. "Henri tried to . . . take something that was mine. I was sick and half-frozen, but he didn't survive his fight with the warrior who was with me. We burned the cabin and left, as soon as I could travel, because we felt sure you'd be back, sooner or later."

"And if you will tell me where you hide the fur of Henri Lavallette, I will allow you to go free," Terrebonne said. Those eyes belied the words, and Cleve knew that the instant he told the Frenchman what he wanted to know, his life was over.

He could only hope to delay these villains long enough to let his wife and Kelly leave the valley and get back to safety in their secret canyon. They had always hidden their trail in order to avoid backtracking from the areas where they were trapping.

Even if the Frenchman found the spot where their rope dangled down the cliff to let them climb back to their route, he doubted that Terrebonne and his henchman could find any track that Second Son intended to hide. Once she was up their line onto the ridge to the east, there was just no way for these villains to locate her.

He drew a deep breath as the man who held him lowered him so that his feet could touch the ground. That one could break his back with one quick move, and he knew it. So he kept his gaze fixed on Terrebonne and thought hard and fast.

"We hid the furs a long way back. We knew we'd be going back along our track, so we stashed them high and dry, but I don't know if I could tell you where, because my wife was the one who picked the spot. I could find it, but I doubt I could give you a map."

The tip of the knife slashed his left cheek. "Do not lie to me. I have scout, Pawnee, who look all the way. They would know, *mon ami*, if someone hide many bale of fur. No, you lie, and I mus' show you what happen when you lie to Jules Terrebonne."

The Frenchman moved toward him, eyes gleaming, knife ready to wreak havoc, Cleve knew. Behind him there was a thunk, and the beefy arms about his shoulders loosed their grip as the body of the man who had held him pitched forward, pushing him off balance.

Cleve fell forward, but he had time to twist aside, and he was not pinned under the huge frame of the other Frenchman. Instead, he shoved the ground away and bounced up, to see the knife flash as Terrebonne threw it.

Cleve turned, time seeming to slow as the blade flew in a shining arc. He had time to note the distant cry of an eagle, the ripple of water in the pond, as he followed the path of the deadly weapon.

"No!" he yelled, moving toward Holy William. "No!" But he seemed mired in quicksand, and he knew he would never be able to stop the deadly steel.

The weapon thunked solidly into the skinny chest of William Kelly, who was standing amid the thin screen of willows along the bank. The skinny preacher's hands clasped about the wooden haft, blood darkening the soiled deerhide of his shirt.

Slowly he sank to his knees, his fingers still trying to pull the metal free of his flesh. He glanced up and his eyes met Cleve's. Pain. Surprise. Was there something like triumph there? Then those eyes glazed over and Holy William fell onto his face in the mud of the pond bank.

Never before had Cleve been known to roar. Now he felt the sound rising in his chest, and it burst from his lips in the heat of his fury. His fingers were extended to choke the life from the man who had killed his friend, but now there was another weapon in those dirty brown hands. Terrebonne must have primed his flintlock earlier, having it ready if it was needed.

There came a roar to make his voice sound feeble, and Cleve felt something strike the side of his head. Blackness flowed through him as he fell again, knowing that this time he had run out his string. This time he was a dead man.

With the last of his consciousness, he heard a shrill war cry. He tried to see, but his vision was gone. *Second Son!* Why hadn't she and Kelly run for the hidden valley?

He struggled frantically to come back from the dark gulf awaiting him, but it was too deep, too black, too bottomless. As he sank into those depths he thought again, with agonized clarity, *My child!*

Then his world went out like a snuffed candle.

chapter

— 17 —

The search for those who were denned up somewhere in the Absarokas had given Jules Terrebonne's
winter more interest than he had expected. His
men were quite capable of trapping their present
range without his supervision. Indeed, he often left
them to their own devices as he roamed the country,
making contact with tribes or traders that might be
useful allies or scouting out other trappers who might
become prey.

He left Yoder in charge, taking Philippe with him.
Usually he traveled alone, but since the loss of his
manhood he felt somehow less self-sufficient. His big
French lieutenant had been a friend for many years

and Terrebonne knew he could trust him with more than his life, at least as long as someone didn't pay too well for a shift in loyalty.

They left the range entirely to move down the snow-crusted valley lying between the Absarokas and the Bighorns. That rock Darnell had described was one Jules had seen, and he had some idea of the general area, but he didn't entirely trust his recollection.

So they retraced the route their prey might have taken. After Philippe returned from a special mission to the country beyond the eastern range with a Pawnee scout, Jules knew that it was only a matter of time before the weasely little scum located the river they wanted.

And it was so. Within a couple of weeks the Pawnee found the rock, the stream, and showed them the route to take in order to get well into the mountains without having to leave their horses behind. As their quarry obviously possessed horses and would take them with him, that route would be the one to follow.

At that point, Jules wanted to send the warrior home with a horse for payment, but he seemed far too interested in learning what they might be seeking. So, instead, Philippe strangled the man and hid his body under a rock slide, cheerfully adding his horse to their string of pack animals.

Terrebonne knew that in winter it was unlikely anyone would come searching for the Pawnee, and by spring the sign would be too blurred by snow and wind to read. No brother warrior would ever find this missing son of the clan, he felt certain.

Besides which, Philippe had spoken to the elders of the scout, Little Badger's, tribe of a trip into the Wind

River Range. They could search there until doomsday without finding anything.

It was blizzard weather by the time they were again well into the Absarokas. Snowslides rampaged down the steep slopes as the pack thickened and winds howled along the canyons, eddying even into the cave where they rode out the worst of the storms.

Only their forethought in loading the pack animals heavily with food kept it from being a hungry winter as well, for it was so bitter that even ermine and snowshoe rabbits didn't venture out of their burrows. Many he knew had frozen or starved in such weather, but Jules knew the country and congratulated himself on being as much a survivor as any Indian ever born.

But at last the big storms eased, and they were able to move deeper into the mountains, between flurries of bad weather. Jules followed the stream until it disappeared into an impassable canyon, at which point he knew that his quarry must have turned aside and crossed some ridge or pass behind his present position.

He must find them before spring thaw opened the ways to the trading fort or the new rendezvous. In order to cover more ground, he and Philippe separated for a time, each of them moving cautiously into valleys, over shoulders of mountains, working their way up the Shadow Mountains.

Areas containing beaver dams were the only ones they checked, searching for snares set in logical spots. In that way they found a great many promising trapping grounds for their own future activities without locating their intended quarry.

At last Philippe returned to their appointed rendezvous with word of a canyon in which he had found traps bearing the scratched *L* that was Henri Lavallette's mark.

"The edge of the cliff, she crumble under my feet," said the big trapper, when at last he appeared after an unusually long absence. "I have leave my horse in little meadow while I scout the land below. By damn, I scout it more than I think, Jules! The edge it fall, and I fall with it, down must be a t'ousand feet or more.

"I say Hail Mary twice while I fall, for I think for certain this be the last minute of my life. Then I go *phoomph!* into snowdrift. My eyes they fill with snow; my mouth she is stop with it. I cannot breathe, for even snow she is ver' hard when you fall so far. But when at last I stop, I am not damage. Not much."

"This drift . . . how deep must it be to keep you from smash on the ground below?" asked Jules, visualizing the scene, the terrible fall, and the providential snowdrift.

"After I tunnel out the side, I stand back and look. That *vache* was forty feet if anyt'ing. I go in like into great feather mattress, *comprends*? And when I get to bottom, I begin to dig. Not up—I know that is too far and the snow will cave in on me.

"I go out, and because of those Hail Mary, perhaps, it is only a few feet and it slope off so I can tumble out. Rock, she have fall off that cliff forever, it seem, and if I have fall ten yards to right or to left, I would be broke to pieces, *mon ami*."

"So you find a trail out and come to me," said Jules. "But what have take you so long?"

"That was not so easy as you say. Once I build fire and melt the snow out of me, I check the pond, and there I find trap. Many trap. They are mark, as I say, with the *L* of Lavallette, and from one I take young beaver and cook meat for strength to find my way out.

"But that I cannot do. That canyon valley, she is long and wide, and I search from end to end. No trail up the cliff can I see, even where deer or chipmunk go up and down. Those cliff, they are tall *canaille*, and low down they are slick as ice.

"Two men, they come into valley on the nex' day, but I know they are there only when I hear voice and I hide. I cannot see how they come, and once they go I cannot find the way. It is like"—his hands waved in frustration—"like they have vanish like the ghost."

"You hide? From only two? *Merde!* That is not like the Philippe I know. Why do you not shoot one and make the other tell you where that trail may be?" Jules felt a sense of astonishment that disturbed him, for he had never seen Philippe intimidated.

"I have lost my flintlock when I fall," the big man said, his tone filled with injured dignity. "I do not dig through that snowdrift again for anything, and I would not find the gun if I do.

"My *grand* knife, she also lose herself from my sheath, and only the *petit* one in my boot is there. The pouch, by the grace of God, remain tie inside my shirt, so I have flint and steel. I am bruise and hurt, stiff, and have not much strength for a long time.

"Beside, those trapper, they know what they do. They watch. They listen. One is *big* fellow, almost as big as me, though the other is tall and thin. I have fall a t'ousand feet, have no weapon, and I want to tell you what I have find. If I am dead, how will you know, *n'est-ce pas?*"

Jules grunted. "So, then, you wait until they go away by these invisible path they use. How do you get out?"

"I find a tall tree. A *sacré grandpère* of a tree that grow up against the southwest wall of that valley. The light, it catch a shadow beside the treetop, and I look close. A ledge, she is there, not so far, maybe.

"Not too far to jump, perhaps, if a man have the courage. And above it is another and another, so that with time and luck, perhaps I climb out." He leaned back on his bedroll and closed his eyes, remembering.

Jules waited patiently. Philippe was an accurate storyteller, but he had to take his time and relive the experience, incident by incident.

"At last I feel strong enough to climb, so I go up that tree like the squirrel. The trunk, she get thinner and thinner, until I think I will not be able to reach that ledge. Yet I do at last, and the top of that great spruce bend and sway under me.

The ledge is . . . eh, perhaps ten feet away, and below there are those terrible rocks, as well as young spruce and pine like the needle, waiting for me to fall. I think a long time, you may be sure, Jules, before I start to sway that spruce, back and forth, many time.

"It whip perhaps five feet this way, five feet that, and when it get as close to that ledge as it will ever do, I kick myself free and fly like the bird to that ledge." He opened his eyes. "May Holy Mary deliver me from ever fly again!"

Terrebonne grunted. "So you climb out, ledge to ledge, like chipmunk. Good thing your horse wait for you. And now we know where they are, if we get down to the bottom. You think you find the way again?"

"I have mark it well, though I have not the eye like you, Jules. The horse, she wait, for there is good grass and much browse where I leave her. So we come to you, though we are gone much longer than I think to be. The sign, she is there."

Terrebonne found that to be true. They had their own system of sign that only those of their company recognized, though some of them might have puzzled an Indian considerably. But the marks were there—a broken branch pointing the direction, a pile of pebbles, a scar on a stone.

As they retraced Philippe's way they went higher and higher into the range. Ahead and above towered stark peaks of black stone streaked with snow. But they turned aside before they came to that forbidding reach of country and at last Philippe gestured for Jules to dismount and join him at a safe distance from the edge of the cliff looking down into that valley.

It was not yet quite spring, and snow lay like frosting beneath the great firs and spruces and pines below. The creek feeding the chain of beaver ponds steamed gently. Terrebonne knew that the water was probably relatively warm, for they were now very near a place he had visited before, years ago. There, water shot from the ground and mud boiled and in winter steam wreathed everything in mist. But here he could see only slight indications of mud pots or steam vents.

Only a gentle line of mist marked the stream, and the dark mounds of lodges in the ponds told him that this held a treasure of beaver. The valley was well wooded, so marten and mink should also be abundant. He would mark this place well once they found a way other than by falling to get down into it, and it would be his.

"The lowest part of the cliff, she is there," said Philippe, pointing past him at a shoulder of stone beside a dark patch, some distance farther along the valley's wall. "With the line we have make, perhaps we get down without we break anything important."

Jules nodded thoughtfully. They had spent several days braiding rawhide rope, using the hides of several deer and a moose they had shot and left to rot, once they secured the skins they needed.

Philippe had kept measuring, in his memory, the distance he had fallen, and not until they had almost a thousand feet of line did he consent to stop. Now the tough rope waited for use, and Terrebonne felt a surge of anticipation.

They turned and led the horses carefully along the edge, keeping well away from the drop. The low point of the cliff was a notch just beyond the shoulder to which Philippe had pointed, and there they found a knob of rock that would belay their line securely.

The descent was both frightening and dangerous, for the top of the cliff overhung the lower walls and there was a tendency to swing back and bash oneself against the stone. Jules went first, concealing the fact that his heart was racing and his lips bitten to keep from crying out as he left the safety of the solid ground.

Stepping off that wall into space was the hardest thing he had ever done in all his life. The abuses of his childhood, the terrible vengeance he had taken upon his enemies, the uncertainty of his voyage to the New World were nothing compared with this. He felt as if he were stepping off into hell itself.

His heart thudding as if to ram its way past his ribs, he cast himself into space. He had made knots in the rawhide and his hands clung desperately as he came to each of them. Even wrapped in deerhide, his palms burned with friction as he slid faster than he had intended toward the bottom of the declivity.

He kicked away from the wall as he swung toward it, swooped outward, forced his desperate fingers to loosen and slide farther, kicked again. This *was* hell, he understood with sudden clarity. He would never reach firm ground again but would swing here between rock and sky for all eternity.

Then his knee hit a boulder, his moccasins found solid earth through a crunchy layer of snow, and he stood upright, favoring the bruised knee and swaying with vertigo and relief.

Philippe seemed to possess no nerves, which Jules had often thought was one aspect of having no brain. He came romping down the cliff as if on a boys' outing, landing beside Terrebonne with a thud.

The big fellow shook himself and snorted. "What you think?" he asked. "We find this by accident. Those other, they likely do the same. No one find it for a ver' long time, and we trap it out, once we find what we seek, eh?"

Terrebonne nodded, half hearing his words. The sun was down behind the western mountain, and those who trapped here would be safely back in their hidden camp. He lifted the pack that anchored the bottom end of the line, which still extended from top to bottom of the cliff, almost invisible against the dark stone. The free end he tied off to a bush, hiding it well.

"We go into trees and hide our supply. Then we scout these country. When those men return, we be ready, eh, *mon ami?*"

They moved cautiously into the thick growth of timber, where spruce and fir cloaked the higher ground, giving way to alder and birch and willow as the soil grew wetter approaching the creeks and ponds. They found a concealed spot beneath the petticoats of a spruce, whose branches came to the ground in a thick green network.

"We will make no fire," said Jules, thinking hard about what must come tomorrow or the next day when those trappers returned to their snares. "They are cautious men, you say. They will smell the smoke, then, and we will not risk that."

Philippe snorted irritably. "*Les pieds,* they are freeze, Jules. How do I warm the feet without fire?"

Terrebonne grunted and said nothing, but once they had eaten their cold ration he rose and made his way up the stream toward the spot where he had seen a light steam rising, as he stood on the rim above. There he found a warm spring trickling from a hole in the rocky wall into a water-worn trench of stone.

"You warm the feet all you like, Philippe, but we do not sleep here. We go back into hide, wrap well in the robes. Before dawn we are up and into position, for now you show me where you find the trap. Then I will know the best way for ambush them."

It was dark before they finished their preparations, and the pair retired under the spruce and dug into the light snow left there to find the mat of needles beneath. A better place to rest would be hard to find in the wild, and Jules eased his bones and sighed as he stretched out in his roll of buffalo robe.

A great satisfaction filled him. Tomorrow he might well learn where Henri's furs were hidden, as well as take vengeance upon the man he suspected of being that enemy back on the Belle Fourche.

chapter

— 18 —

The route to the trapping valley was difficult even before she became so heavy with child, but Second Son was determined to make one last trip there before the birth. Getting out of their own valley was not easy, and letting herself down the rawhide line they carried with them, each time, for descending into that other sheer-walled canyon and climbing back out again would tax her, she knew, to her utmost.

That was her intention. Now she knew why few women became warriors. As long as one remained celibate, it was good. One had freedom to go and come, to hunt and steal horses and ride with the band to war. Once pregnant, everything became much harder. The body changed its center of balance, the legs had to compensate for greater weight, and even the most ordinary task became a challenge to strength and innovative skills.

Yet she had never slacked her efforts as the child grew. Her people knew that maintaining strength and energy was often the difference between survival and death.

Second Son had no intention of becoming soft and lazy, as a few women she had known allowed themselves to become. So as she followed Kelly up the intricate way she took pride in never falling behind, never risking herself to foothold or handgrip until she was certain it would sustain her increased weight. Her ability to continue such activities was necessary, she knew, if she was to be a partner to Yellow Hair.

Once they reached the ridge she paused to sniff the air, as was her invariable custom. Nothing but the steamy scent of hot springs and the tang of conifers reached her nostrils. The air was so clear and clean that it almost intoxicated her, and she felt, inside, the strong stirring of the child, disturbed by her exertions.

The descent on the line was harder than ever before, but she said nothing; by the time they went about their business she felt full of energy. Suddenly she seemed able to do anything at all, whatever her physical predicament, and she enthusiastically began checking the traps in her sector.

"Kelly!" The cry shocked her upright. The drowned beaver in the trap was forgotten as she slid her knife into her hand and slipped into the screen of leafless trees between her position and the forest.

She could hear hurried steps crunching toward

Cleve's position, and she wanted desperately to run after Holy William, for she had never heard Yellow Hair call for help in that way before. Yet some instinct told her that this was no ordinary disaster that had overtaken him.

There were strangers in this valley, she knew with sudden sureness. They had built no fire to betray their presence; they had made no sound. But this was an ambush, though how it could have happened in this inaccessible place she could not imagine.

She went deep into the trees, taking a curving course toward the noises that now came to her ears. A fight was going on, a desperate struggle that was crashing and crunching amid bushes and grass. She leaped from foothold to foothold, crossing the stream to come around toward the spot from which the sounds were coming.

Before she arrived, she could hear voices, Cleve's tense and harsh, the other too familiar. That was Terrebonne! She stopped in her tracks, her heart going chill and hard.

Her knife became like a part of her hand, and when she moved it was with the relentless motion of an avalanche. Terrebonne!

Cleve's roar told her that something terrible had happened, and she sped on, almost there now. The sound of a shot added momentum, but before she came into sight of the spot from which the noise had come she slid through the brush edging the stream, finding the end of the dam and going cautiously around it, to stand at the pond, concealed for a moment to assess the situation.

Terrebonne's back was to her, and he was gazing at the limp body of Holy William, which had dropped like a discarded robe onto the damp soil. Nearer to the Frenchman was another shape that could only be Cleve, lying ominously still; behind him was yet another, a huge bulk of a man who was kicking and groaning, trying to rise to his feet.

"Be still, Philippe," said Terrebonne in French. She remembered enough to understand the words as her old enemy bent over his friend. "You are hurt ver' bad. It is best, perhaps, if you do not suffer."

She saw the swift motion of the knife that he had retrieved from Holy William's body. The coppery scent of blood filled the air, and the big man twitched as the blade was thrust into his chest.

She moved, not feeling her weight, not feeling the infant moving desperately in her belly, not thinking of danger but only of vengeance. If he had killed her man, he would not live to boast of it.

But she was no fool. He had his rifle in his hands, reloaded now, and she had no intention of risking her child. She screamed like a cougar and staggered artfully into the clearing, clutching her belly, her knife hidden inside the slit she had cut into her robe.

Dropping to her knees, she groaned, still holding her distended stomach in her hands, as if in the throes of childbirth. She kept Terrebonne in sight, though she tried her best to conceal that. When he came close enough to see her face, she heard him catch his breath.

There came a thick chuckle. "I think I see the small warrior who remove *mes testicules, n'est-ce pas?*" He tramped closer and laid his rifle aside, leaning it carefully against a willow.

"And now you are *très enciente* and unable to protect yourself, *ma petite.* You would not accommodate me, *non!* You mus' wait for thees *cochon* and lie with him!

And now he is dead, with rifle ball where his brain should be, and you are belong to me."

He stepped forward and caught her braid, tugging her head up to make her look into his eyes. "I cannot serve you as I should, for you remove that power from me. But before I am done, you will think long about the mistake you make when you castrate Jules Terrebonne!"

Second Son closed her eyes so he would not read her purpose there. She sobbed convincingly and fell forward when he released her hair, curling about the child protectively.

She felt the vibration of his steps as he moved around her, surveying the scene, making certain that no one lived who might help her. But there was no sound, and in her heart she began to grieve for Yellow Hair, lying so near her and yet so inaccessible in death. Fury belt steadily and her muscles tensed for what must come next.

At last the cautious Frenchman came near and bent over her. She faced away from him as he stood at the curve of her back and kept herself motionless with terrible effort. Through her lashes, she saw his dirty face bend past her shoulder, peer at her as if assessing her ability to defend herself, and disappear.

He would come, she knew, for she willed it with all the intensity of her being. He would think to strip her, tie her to a post driven into the damp soil of this valley, and take from her all dignity, all courage, and eventually her life, at the point of his knife or with the help of fire. She knew how that was done, for so her people served those who deserved such a fate.

She gripped the haft of the knife through the slit, waiting, holding herself ready as Terrebonne's footsteps came around and there was the sound of his knees sinking into mud. Hands caught her shoulders and shook her, pulling her up into a kneeling position.

She kept her eyes closed as she allowed him to lift her to her knees. He slapped her hard, making her head rock, her ears ring, but she refused to open them. Again he struck her, this time loosing his grip a bit.

Now! It was time!

Second Son, warrior of the Burning Heart Band of the Tsistsistas, opened her eyes and grinned into the face of the Frenchman. Before he could react, her hands came up, and the knife was digging its point into his throat at the notch of his collarbone.

She was facing him now, one hand ready to counter any move he might make, the other holding the knife. Terrebonne's hands moved away from her body as if she burned him. She knew the Frenchman was seeking for some weapon to use that would not endanger his jugular, and she tensed to thrust the blade home. Something moved at the edge of her vision, but she didn't take her gaze from the livid face of the thief.

Then she was sure—one of those dead men had risen to his feet, only a few yards from Terrebonne's back. Which? Distracted, she failed to finish her thrust.

Terrebonne, seeing the shift in her gaze, moved to strike away her blade, but before he could complete the motion, Cleve had crossed the narrow space between them and his hands caught Jules around the neck from behind.

"Yellow Hair!" she said. "You live!" She felt a great smile welling up inside her as she rose to her feet with some difficulty and regarded her bloodied husband.

"No thanks to this bastard," he said, shaking Terrebonne as if he were a child. "I'm going to put him out of his misery. Serve him right. He got poor old William, after the preacher saved my life."

She saw the Frenchman's eyes widen until the whites showed all around. He gulped audibly, and she thought of the terrible things he had done that she knew about. How many far more terrible ones had there been that she did not know?

She shook her head. "I think this is too clean, too quick for him. He has made others suffer, I know from the tales I have heard. Tie him. Then we will decide what he deserves."

There was a sudden strangeness inside her, as if, far away, a signal cry had been given for a battle. Her entire body seemed to be waiting, preparing for what was to come, and she knew with sudden finality that the child would be born now, far from their familiar tipi and the soft hides she had dressed to wrap him in.

But nothing was ever easy, in her experience, and she felt no alarm. A child would be born. He would live or die, as would she. The thing was to make ready and to secure this prisoner so that he would not escape before he was dealt with fairly.

"I think I must go into the trees," she said, her tone formal, as was fitting at such a moment. A man should not be disturbed by the processes of birth, for though men fought and gained wounds with great pride, the things that occurred to bring an infant into the world seemed to horrify them.

Cleve looked surprised. "Right now? We've got to decide what to do about this bastard before we do anything else. . . ."

At that moment her water broke, and a flood of liquid darkened her robe and her moccasins. He looked down, then up into her eyes.

She nodded. "It is time, Yellow Hair. Tie this one so that he can barely breathe, and sit close to watch him. Make fire, if you will, for I may be chilled when I return."

He opened his mouth to protest; among his kind there was much concern with helping the woman giving birth, and she knew he wanted to go with her, to help in any way he could, but that would not be fitting. If, at the moment, she was not a Cheyenne warrior, she was, to her bones, a Cheyenne woman. Such behavior on the part of her child's father would disgrace her.

As she turned toward the trees Cleve knocked their prisoner on the head with the haft of the knife he had taken from her hand. She smiled, knowing that when Terrebonne awoke, he would be bound for good and all.

Then she sobered, knowing that they would miss Holy William as they went on with their lives. He had longed to see the child, wanting to do the ritual of his people over the infant. Now he never would.

She gasped as a long contraction shook her, and her legs refused to move for a long moment. When her muscles unlocked, she went beneath a spreading fir tree and dug down into the needles, making a shallow pit over which she squatted, breathing evenly.

The control that she had learned with every beat of her heart took over. She waited patiently as the muscles of her body, knowing what to do, went through the process of bringing her child into the light of this day.

The squeezing pains changed to long ones running down her body. She could feel the child moving, moving, and when the head reached the proper position, she pushed with all her might. With a rush the child was delivered, and she reached beneath and took him out of the nest of fir needles.

The infant gasped as she bit the cord in two and tied a knot in the length still attached to him. Then she squeezed his small body between her hands until he drew breath and gave a mewing cry.

She unrolled a length of her robe, and on that she laid him while she tended the afterbirth and covered it in the hole she had dug. After padding herself with soft leather from her pouch, she wiped the blood and fluids from his skin and took him inside her deerhide shirt, binding a length of thong beneath his weight to hold him in place.

She had to rest for a time, leaning back amid the fragrant needles, drawing deep breaths and ignoring the soreness left in her body. That would go away. For now, she and Yellow Hair had a strong son, who was even at that early moment nuzzling at her breast.

chapter
— 19 —

Cleve's face was crusted with dried blood that he had been too busy to wash off. The throbbing in his head was matched only by his anger at this arrogant Terrebonne, who assumed that anything he wanted was his by some divine right of strength and brutality.

As hard as he tried, Cleve couldn't quite recall what it was that had brought him out of unconsciousness after the rifle ball glanced along his skull and knocked him out. Perhaps it was some instinct, deeper than any he had ever suspected he might possess, that warned him his wife and child were in danger. Or maybe, as Holy William might have said, it was the hand of God.

As he dug in the soft soil beyond the creek, where the warm springs below the earth kept it workable, he wondered about that. Who would have thought this morning, setting off together in bright sunlight and bracing chill, that tonight he would be burying the skinny little man who had begun as a rescued captive and ended as a friend?

Philippe was a villain he would not bother to touch or to bury. Let the wolves that howled on the heights come down and feed off his bones. He did not deserve anything from the man he had almost helped to kill. His corpse was only a dark blur, around which Cleve stepped without glancing at it.

But William was going to have decent burial, and Cleve recalled enough of the words of the service to say something fitting over him, too. God knew, if there were any truth to Him at all, that this was the only way, in this wild land, to send a man to his reward.

So he chose a spot beneath a fair-sized tree near the pond, for that would be shady in summer. He finished the grave as neatly as he could and carried the light body of his friend to the site. Cleve gently closed the eyelids over Kelly's staring eyes. Then he lifted the body again and stepped down into the grave to arrange the preacher straight, with his hands properly folded. Ma had always done that with bodies of neighbors when she was called to help at a death.

It took a while to fill in the grave, but once that was done, he tied two straight branches together to make a crude cross and stuck it into the ground at the head of the disturbed ground. Then he stepped back and looked down sadly.

Knowing that such rituals meant nothing to Second Son, he didn't wait for her to return. He bowed his head and said words that now, so far from Pa and his cruel uses of religion, began to mean something again.

That wicked-eyed buffalo, back there on the Missouri, was receding into the past, along with Cleve's terrible sense of guilt. Now he was a husband, about to be a father.

He was a man who could wrest his living from this wild country, brave the Shadow Mountains, eliminate a band of enemies. He had survived things that would have sent him into spasms to think of, back when he was a child on the Little Sac River.

He tamped the dirt level and began bringing rocks from the area beneath the frowning cliff to cover the preacher's grave. With at least half his mind he worried about Second Son, who had disappeared into the spruces and now made no sound to indicate if she lived or not.

He had been at Cousin Lily's house with Ma once when a baby was born. He recalled with much clarity the moans, the rushing about with towels and water, the frantic scream from his cousin, and the thin wail that followed it, behind the closed door of the big bedroom.

It was now almost dark. The day had passed in such a succession of violent and dramatic events that he could hardly believe it was already so late. He heaved the last load of rocks onto the long thin scar of raw earth that covered Holy William Kelly, who had not been treated well by anyone in all his life, until the very end of it.

Once he had the grave fixed to suit him, he took from William's possibles bag the ornate head of that dead warrior who had tormented the little man and set it upright on the pile of rocks. There was something strangely fitting about having that grisly specimen guard the preacher's last resting place.

As he straightened there came a faint gurgling cry from the depths of the wood. He tensed, waiting to see if Second Son would emerge, but she didn't, and the canyon grew darker.

Far above, there was a loud howl, echoing down the valley and off the cliffs until it sounded like a pack of wolves, instead of a lone wolf crying to the night. At the edge of hearing there came an answer from some distant animal, and on the heels of that the moon rose in a halo of cloud above the eastern height.

His fire, which had died down while he buried Kelly, was only a mass of red gold, marked with charred wood stubs. He went into the edge of the wood and dragged up dead branches, wet with snow, that sputtered and steamed as he arranged them in tipi fashion over the coals.

Then he went to the traps he had dropped so long before and took them up. He retrieved every one within hearing range of his fire, for he didn't want to miss hearing if Second Son should call. In one was a fat young beaver.

He finished with all the nearby traps before retiring to the fire and preparing beaver tail to roast on sharpened sticks over the deep coals at its edge. Cleve arranged fresh branches of spruce and fir, making a couch before the blaze. Then he sat on the fragrant heap, waiting with impatience and growing alarm. When would his wife walk out of the trees, carrying his child?

Kelly had insisted that it must be a son, but Cleve had found, somewhat to his chagrin, that he didn't really care. He liked Second Son so much that he had no objection to having a smaller version of her about his camp, clinging to his robe, making water on his lap, as the infants back in the Burning Heart village had done.

From time to time he went over to the bound shape of Terrebonne and looked down into his eyes, which glared up with insane hatred from the muddy face. He had gagged the Frenchman with a thong and a bit of willow wood so he could do nothing but grunt.

Cleve didn't understand French curses very well, for it had been a long time since he traveled the Missouri with Ashworth's Frenchmen. But the noise became irritating at last and he had decided to stop the flow.

Again he added fuel to the fire, stopping to trickle water around Terrebonne's gag as he passed. He might be about to kill this thief in a cruel and painful manner, but until then he kept thinking of the buffalo bull with frosted horns. That was something that a man with that totem would do. He preferred not to become such a man.

He would kill, if necessary. He would punish someone who threatened his family and killed his friend, but by God he would not lower himself to the level of this Frenchman.

When he had given up hope entirely and was preparing to seek out his dead wife and child and give them burial beside Holy William, Second Son appeared between two young spruces, a shadow striped with flickering light from the fire.

She carried a bundle wrapped inside her shirt and held with a thong, which tied her robe close to her body. Her face was drawn and pale, even in the rosy light.

He rose, feeling a great relief. "You are all right?"

he asked her, moving cautiously to touch her shoulder.

"All is well," she said, her face grave and weary yet strangely beautiful. "We have a son." She reached to touch his sleeve, tentatively, as if she had come back from some distant place and hardly knew him.

Cleve looked down at the tiny bundle in her arms. "Is it all right with you if we call him Bill? I want to give him a Cheyenne name, but I'd really like to call him after Holy William, for a nickname."

Second Son untied the thong, took the child from her breast, and handed him to his father. "I, too, liked the little man. We will call him Bill, if you want."

"But I would like to give him another name, Wolf Sings on the Mountain. I heard the brother crying on the height, earlier. My own brother knows, I think, out there on the plains, that I have a son, and that was his greeting to us."

She sank wearily onto the pile of fragrant branches and stretched out her feet to the flames. "Are you pleased, Yellow Hair, with your son?"

Cleve hunkered down beside her and held the warm, damp shape of the infant. In the firelight he could see wisps of dark hair curving over the small round skull. The tiny face was soft-featured, the nose a round button, the eyes squinched so tightly that the lids didn't show.

Even as he gazed the dark eyes opened and stared up as if memorizing the features of this newfound father. The child made a tiny grunting sound, and the lips worked as if seeking nourishment already. It was the most beautiful child he had ever seen, and a sense of pride and fear filled Cleve as he unconsciously clasped the child closer.

Bill began to cry. Second Son reached to take the

infant back, pushing him under the tail of her shirt so small Wolf Sings on the Mountain could suckle again.

"What do we do with that one?" Cleve asked, nodding toward their bound captive. "I'm afraid if we don't kill him, he'll come after us again. We can't have that—the son of a bitch wouldn't hesitate to kill a baby."

"There is a way," said Second Son. "It is cruel. It is not honorable. But I have known it to be done to enemies who deserved neither the kindness of death nor the honor of torture.

"The punishment is great and the suffering terrible." She rocked her body gently in that manner that women seem to acquire at once, without being taught, when they hold a baby. From beneath her shirt came a soft hiccup.

As she spoke Cleve wondered how she could be so tender and so merciless at the same moment; he felt revulsion, followed by a growing sense that this would be justice, if anything might be. When she was done, he nodded, though he looked no more toward the shape of Terrebonne.

They rested beside the fire all night, preparing for the journey back to their hidden camp. Cleve gathered all the traps in the first light of morning, attached them in bunches to the hanging line they left for climbing up the wall on the eastern side of the valley, and hauled them to the top of the cliff. He hated leaving Second Son and Bill in the company of Terrebonne, tied though he might be, for the place where the rope was secured was distant from the fire. Yet he had to do that, before tackling the rest of the tasks in store.

They had more beaver, and Second Sun skinned

them out while he was gone. Cleve raised those plews in the same manner to the top of the valley wall. By the time that was done, Second Son had boiled more beaver tail in the pot that Holy William always carried with him, no matter how short the journey. Cleve ate the meat and Second Son drank the broth to build up her strength.

He could see energy pouring back into her as she ate, and when she rose to prepare the infant for travel, some elasticity had returned to her step. She paused beside the fire and looked down at their captive before moving away into the concealing trees in a deceptive direction that did not seem to lead toward their skinny ladder leading out.

"Jules Terrebonne," Cleve said, "you have done terrible things to many people, for I have heard the tales. My brother-in-law welcomed you to our band after Second Son saved you from freezing, and you returned that kindness by trying to rape her. Now you will suffer, as you should."

Second Son had disappeared through the low-flung branches of spruces, alders, and birches, leaving Cleve to finish this terrible task alone. As he approached the recumbent man Cleve saw his eyes widen until the whites were once again pale circles in that grubby face.

Terrebonne chewed at his gag, squirmed in his bonds, but Cleve had learned long ago to bind a man so that he could never wriggle loose. First Emile Prevot, that most effective of teachers in Ashworth's band, and then Cub, Second Son's nephew, had given him instruction in the art. One whom the Cheyenne bound did not escape without help.

He caught the trapper by his hair and tugged him to a sitting position. Then, with cruel deliberation, he chose a slender tree very near the water's edge and at the foot of William's grave and trimmed its lower branches to the height of his own head. The stripped trunk gleamed pale in the morning light.

When he returned to the embers of the fire, Terrebonne stared at him with terrified speculation, but Cleve said nothing. Instead, he hauled him up by his bound arms and frog-marched him toward the birch.

The coil of rawhide line dangling from the thongs at his waist weighed heavily as Cleve walked, but he pushed the thought of what he was about to do into the very back of his mind. He deliberately thought of other matters, putting his mother, his wife, and his son out of his consciousness.

Concentrating on the Frenchman instead, he pushed him against the tree, turned him about, and began binding him tightly to the slender bole. Shoulders, waist, neck, knees, ankles, hips, he wrapped the flexible rawhide around and around, until the man could do nothing but open and close his eyes.

Then he cut the thong binding the gag in Terrebonne's mouth. The trapper licked his lips with a dry tongue, tried to speak and spat instead, though evidently his mouth was so dry that nothing came out but air.

"American!" he croaked, and the word was a curse. "You burn me, eh?"

"No." Cleve took his skinning knife from its sling and tried the blade against a switch of willow. It sliced through cleanly.

He approached the bound man. Cutting between the bindings, he sliced away robe, trousers, moccasins, until only what was confined beneath the raw-

hide was left on the pale, blue-pimpled body of the
Frenchman.

Stepping away, he regarded his handiwork criti-
cally. "You have supplies someplace nearby, I know,
but I have no time to search. It'll be even worse for
you, knowing you have a bedroll and food someplace
here and not being able to get to it."

"What do you do?" howled Terrebonne.

"Why nothing," said Cleve. "Nothing at all. What
I'm going to do I've done. Now I'm going home with
my wife and my son, and you're going to stay here all
by yourself." He felt a wicked smile wrinkle his face.

"It's too warm down here among the hot springs for
you to freeze to death very fast, but it's too cold for
you to live very long, either. You'll starve or die
for lack of water, or you'll chill too much to survive.
One or the other'll get you, if the wolves don't come
down off the ridges and get to you first.

"It's the wondering that'll do for you as much as the
pain and the cold, I'd think. You're going to hear
every marten moving in the woods, every beaver
splashing in the pond there, and it'll make your bones
shake, thinking what it might be. When the wolf
howls or a cougar screams, you're just going to know
you're going to be its next meal."

He glanced about to see that nothing was near that
might offer escape to the man tied to the tree. Only
the dead lump that was Philippe could be seen. Then,
without another word, he turned back toward the
dying coals of the fire, which he kicked out and
stamped into the soil.

"You cannot do this to me!" came the cry from the
edge of the beaver pond. "I am Jules Terrebonne! I
have men who will come and destroy you and your

woman and your *enfant*!" But the words held more rage than hope.

Cleve hoisted his last pack and slipped through the trees to the rawhide line that he must climb in the pale light of this overcast morning. The sky promised snow. That might finish off the thief sooner than he'd like, but he knew that he would never have come up with as suitable a torture for Terrebonne as his wife had done.

He reached the rope and began to climb, seeing above him the dark shape of Second Son silhouetted against the sky. As he went up the line, swinging gently and sweating with exertion, his son began to make soft sounds, and he redoubled his efforts.

Today they would return home to their little valley and their warm tipi. Today they would begin their lives as a family. Cleve gritted his teeth, the rope cutting into his hands, but when he reached the top, he was smiling.

Today was going to be fine, for the sun was rising beyond the trees atop the ridge.

chapter
— 20 —

Never had Jules been so afraid. Why had he pursued those two, who had been nothing but misfortune each time he had met them? He wondered desperately about that as he struggled to work his hands free or kick his feet loose.

Was this how De Brassis had felt, all those years ago, when he was pursued and caught by the peasants he had tormented as if they were animals without feeling? For an instant Jules saw the face of the child, the mouth a square of agony, as he drove the spike through his soft belly. He saw the face of the father, watching helplessly as his son was destroyed.

Now Terrebonne shivered with cold and terror.

Was there, after all, some remote God, as the *père* had said, who took vengeance with his own hands upon those breaking His law?

But no. The priest had been a cruel beast. It had not been God but men who punished him for his crimes.

Again Terrebonne squirmed, pushed, arched his back against the cruel rawhide that held him in its clammy embrace. The wolf, high on the ridge above this inaccessible place, gave a cry that echoed up and down the glen. As if in answer, Jules groaned, rivaling the beast in anguish.

He turned his gaze toward his fallen comrade. If only he had not given Philippe the coup de grace, perhaps the big man might have roused himself and cut his leader loose. Why had he had that misplaced impulse to do the man a kindness? That was very foreign to Terrebonne's nature!

Only random sparks were left of the blaze that the American had covered, but in the intense darkness those were enough to show him the dead lump that had been the only friend he had ever made among his henchmen.

At his feet was a rough mound, covered with rocks from the cliff. The thin fellow who killed his friend lay there at his feet. It was not what he had expected when he threw that knife, for he had thought to exult over the survivors before he bore them thoughtfully and painfully into death. Now he would die slowly, agonizingly, while that one was already free of his pain.

Something moved in the little clearing. A predator, already gnawing at the body of poor Philippe. The stars winked above the treetop, and the ridge was outlined in black against the spangled sky. A vast loneliness filled the place, and its chill went deep into Terrebonne's soul, filling him with fear, for he was not fit, this one, to go before God.

Again he struggled, kicked, chewed at the rawhide he could reach. That, at least, began to give a bit, and he gnawed until his mouth ran with blood, his teeth ached.

When at last the thong fell away, he spat out the scraps of leather and wood and tried to find some moisture on his tongue. Thirst was going to be the worst of it, he thought.

Hunger he could endure and had many times over the years. But already his throat felt as if it cracked, and his tongue was thick from the leather and willow-root gag.

The stars shifted overhead, and he was shivering with the cold. Again the wolf howled, and he thought of the sounds De Brassis had made, there before his great house, in the company of those who had been his chattels. Had he suffered like this?

Guilt was not a thing that Jules had ever allowed to trouble him, but now he felt a twinge of something painful and immediate. He squeezed his eyes shut and tried to recall a prayer. Not the Paternoster or the Ave Maria that the priest had taught him but a little verse his mother sang to him when he was very small.

He had lost the words amid the rivers of blood that had washed through his life. Only the tune rang in his head, and his lips were too dry to sing, even if he had the inclination.

Instead he heard the slip-slop of a beaver leaving the pond. The wet body trailed over the grave in front of Terrebonne, its breath sounding loud in the stillness. The rocks covering the mound rattled as it fumbled its way over this unaccustomed obstacle.

"Philippe, live!" he begged the dead man. "Breathe! Come to life and free your old *ami*, will you not?" But the dead man did not stir, and the beaver went on its way, until after a time he heard the quiet sound of its teeth on wood.

"Merciful God," he began. Then he stopped and bit his lip.

Never had he begged for mercy, no matter how harsh the pain, how terrible the punishment. Even when De Brassis cut off his finger, and he was only a child at the time, he had not cried.

No, Jules Terrebonne did not beg for mercy. If the flames of hell awaited him, then he would go into them as the man he had formed himself to be. Cruelty was the thing he had always known and had clung to as the one stable fact of his life.

This was a cruel death, which, perhaps, was fitting. Was this what his old enemy had felt, there before the carven door of his house in the *valleé* de Brassis? This cold certainty that all his strength, all his wit, all his accumulated experience could do nothing to save him?

No wonder the man had gone to his death with his face wet with tears. No wonder he had seemed to welcome that last moment, instead of resisting it.

Terrebonne looked up again. A new strip of stars hung above the glen where the stream ran and the beaver labored to make fur for trappers yet to come.

Those who were his enemies would come here again, find his bones still bound to this tree, and laugh at the defeat of Jules Terrebonne, *Français*, leader of men, harsh master and cruel foe. Or others would come and wonder who this might be, standing between the remnants of Philippe's bones and the rockbound grave of the thin American.

What did it matter? Again the wolf howled.

This time, despite his painful throat, his hopeless situation, Jules raised his own voice in the little song whose words now came back to him.

"Dans les jardins du ciel, le Bon Dieu . . ."

Did He indeed wait for good children in the gardens of heaven? Jules felt sadly that he would never know.

AFTERWORD

Although it may seem strange to those who like to think of early trappers in the West as nature's noblemen, there were among them those who preyed upon their own kind. Any group of human beings, it seems, produces bad apples.

Jules Terrebonne is French, not because I think the French would be more likely than others to do such things but because that background gives him more years in trapping country and sound motivation for what he does as a predator. The revolution in France loosed upon the world many embittered people.

The furs gathered by those engaged in trapping were valuable items for trade or sale. It was far easier to steal what another man had spent years of back-breaking labor to gather than it was to do the work yourself. This was probably not widespread, for there were very few white trappers spread over an immense expanse of plains and mountains, but it did happen. Probably the most successful raids were those whose victims did not live to spread the word.

A lot of the early history of the Great Plains and the mountain regions was written by early French explorers and trappers. Those who read that language often find that matters which have been misconstrued or misinterpreted concerning the tribes can be resolved by reading those early accounts, for they were written before dislocations and contaminations of those cultures by American infiltration into the area. The French accounts, in fact, tend to be more accurate than those of the incoming Americans.

The existence of women warriors is documented fact. The existence of men who took female roles is also well established, and the word *berdache,* which has been taken to mean "homosexual," alluded to such role changes. However, the person involved often took this course in life as the direct result of his medicine dream or vision in adolescence. It did not represent personal orientation so much as a "choice by the gods" that he or she must obey. Second Son, however, became a warrior simply because her people recognized her strengths and skills and took advantage of them for the good of the tribe.

According to some historians' calculations, only about sixteen out of any hundred men going out to become mountain men survived after a year in the wild. Who knows how many of those might have fallen victim to their own kind?

Of course, sickness was also a killer, and from the different tribes the trappers learned various treatments for common ills. The bark of the common willow, found throughout the United States, is a source of salicylic acid, which is the base ingredient for aspirin.

It was widely used among Native Americans as a painkiller and as a means of breaking fevers. Dosages were uneven, and unbuffered salicylic acid sometimes had unexpected side effects.

There was a veritable pharmacopoeia of medicinal herbs, many of which would probably be beneficial in modern-day medicine, if examined closely. For every ill there was an herbal treatment, some of which were most effective.

If they survived and trapped with some success, the trappers had to dispose of their catch. Making the long and perilous journey back to St. Louis every year or two was a terrible waste of time, as well as being risky.

Very early in the nineteenth century, Manuel Lisa established a trading fort at the point where the Bighorn River joins the Yellowstone. This venture was extremely profitable for many years until William Ashley's rendezvous plan in the early 1820s made it more convenient for trappers to converge each year in a predetermined spot for trading and carousing.

The location changed each year, but the very first was held at Henry's Fork on the Green River, near the present Utah–Wyoming border, in 1825.

Of course, the Native Americans in the mountains and the plains had their own traditions and histories. Their tribal skirmishes became oral tradition, some of which is still in existence.

The battle mentioned by Second Son between the Shoshone and the Crow is based loosely upon the Battle of Crowheart Butte. I have set this conflict much earlier than the real one, but such a battle actually was fought, and there is a marker along the highway leading north between the Absaroka and Wind River ranges commemorating it.

Barbarism was very much a part of life in that time and place. Whether among red people or white, the sort of kind and caring mind-set cultivated in the latter half of the twentieth century was as yet undreamed of. Religions of all kinds taught fear and guilt, rather than love, and torture was not something that only primitive peoples indulged in.

Europe was as barbaric, in its way, as any of the Indian nations, and those individuals coming out of the Old World fitted nicely into the younger barbarisms of the New. So it is not strange that vengeance might involve torture and death, either for white men or red.

Neither is it unusual in the history of mankind that women, even though charged with the nurture of the young, might take out their frustrations and hostilities in torturing the bodies of enemies. That was a different time, with people whose emotions were focused on different matters.

The plains have been broken to the plow or devastated by grazing cattle, who do not move on and let the grass grow again. The mountains are being timbered, quarried, tunneled, and troubled by the workings of our kind. Our cities are disaster areas from which most who are able to do so are fleeing.

To one who wants to escape to a time that had more freedom, more danger and cruelty, and yet a strange kind of cleanliness, a return to the era of the mountain man can come as a pleasure and a relief.

If you enjoyed
THE UNTAMED
by John Killdeer,
be sure to look for the next novel in his
MOUNTAIN MAJESTY
series,
WILDERNESS RENDEZVOUS,
available soon wherever Bantam titles are sold.

* * *

Turn the page for an exciting preview of
WILDERNESS RENDEZVOUS,
Book 3 in the MOUNTAIN MAJESTY series
by John Killdeer.

chapter
— 1 —

The timber wolf was lank with winter, his ribs straining at his hide, his eyes sick and rheumy. Starvation stalked at his heels, and he had hunted in vain for a rabbit or a chipmunk that had ventured out to search for an early sprig of grass.

When he scrabbled down the edge of the waterfall into the narrow valley, he was wavering on his legs, but a sound in the distance sent a surge of adrenaline through him. Ears pricking up, he turned toward the source of that thin wail. Some infant animal was there, and in his present condition that was all he was able to handle.

His teeth gleamed in the pale light, his tongue lolling from the corner of his muzzle. With dogged determination, he set out for the source of the cry, even though the tang of smoke told him that a predator more dangerous than he might be very close by.

The wind sweeping down the narrow valley was chilled with snow, yet it held a faint scent that was a promise of spring as well. Cleve Bennett, stepping out of the tipi he shared with his wife and son, gazed through the stinging flakes and the dim dawn light, seeking some break in the clouds. Here in the mountain heights it seemed like winter, but he knew that down in the lower country spring had lit the valleys with blossom and greened them with grass.

The tribes, Absaroka, Kiowa, Shoshone, Blackfoot, would be hunting, raiding for horses, stirring their winter-sluggish blood to action. It was going to be an interesting spring, for at present his family had as many plews as their horses could carry, and it was time to leave the safety of their valley to market them. That was going to be dangerous business.

He was thinking about the information he had obtained from Jules Terrebonne, trapper and fur thief. Cleve's former employer in the Rocky Mountain Fur Company, William Ashworth, was arranging to bring trappers and traders together at a rendezvous in early summer, where the harvest of the past winters' trapping could be sold or traded. This would save Cleve and Second Son the long journey back east to sell their furs, or the trek to the trading fort, where they were almost certain to be cheated.

It was to begin in June, and Cleve rummaged through his memory, trying to find what date this might be in the calendar he had left behind some years ago when he left Missouri. His first winter was spent on the Missouri River, forted up while Ashworth returned to St. Louis to replace the horses that had been stolen by Indians. The trappers had left there when the river thawed. Had that been April? Or was it late March?

As he recalled each of the incidents sticking in his memory over the past seasons, he made another mark. With those as indicators, he should be able to be accurate as to the year, if not the actual month.

He counted his marks. It had to be 1825. If they had arrived here by August, there had been . . . one, two . . . three . . . He counted moons, and then he realized that there were weeks and weeks when they had seen no glimpse of sky.

Second Son was no help, for the Cheyenne used a different system for keeping track of seasons. Even her monthly periods were of no use, for she'd been pregnant all that time.

He spat into a patch of snow, now dirty and draggled,

and drew a deep breath. The fragrance of pine and spruce, the faint sulfurous tang from the hot springs, the clean scent driving down the wind from the west filled him with a sense of well-being.

It had to be at least late April, though they still had storms that brought heavy snow to the surrounding peaks and ridges, falling mostly as rain in their almost inaccessible valley. Occasional snowslides off the steep cliffs reminded them how lucky they were to be sheltered in this spot. Even the occasional scouting Crow or Blackfoot had not troubled them in their winter quarters.

His dog Snip sniffed at his ankle, wagged his tail hopefully, and stared toward a patch of firs. He almost whined, though Snip seldom made a noise at all.

Cleve heard a faint gurgle from the thicket, but he deliberately didn't look in that direction. Cheyenne ways of raising a baby were so different from any he had ever known that they made him fiercely uncomfortable.

"Babies are supposed to cry!" he'd yelled at Second Son the first time, while she bundled their week-old son onto his cradleboard and started for the doorflap.

She turned her dark eyes on him with an expression of scorn. "You would risk your family, your furs, and your life to allow a baby to cry? This is not acceptable. He will learn, as I did and all my kind, not to make any noise.

"Yellow-Hair, this is the way of my people necessary for survival. I will not die because my son is undisciplined, and neither will you." She glanced down at the fur-wrapped bundle in her arms. "And neither will he."

She had stalked out, carrying the baby in her arms, board and all, and he had followed to see what she was going to do. She didn't spank the child or scold him. Instead, she took him some distance from the tipi, checked the area for any possible danger, and hung the board by its thongs high in a tree on the downwind side.

Young Billy-Wolf began howling lustily, but his mother turned her back and returned to the tipi, shooing her doubtful man before her. The cries behind them rose in volume as the two moved out of eyeshot and into the tipi. Cleve felt as if he were abandoning his child to the elements.

"For Chrissakes, woman, that baby will go crazy, left out there to himself. You cuddle a baby that cries. That's the way my ma did me and my brothers. Or Pa whopped us." He sat on a pile of furs and stuffed his fingers into his ears so he couldn't hear the faint wails.

Second Son sat beside him and jerked his hands down so he could hear her. "There is work to do. We must make new moccasins before we go to this trading council. We do not want to be shamed before all those other white men because we are shabby. Here, set your foot on this."

She stretched a layer of dressed deerhide on the floor and touched his knee. Sighing, Cleve moved his foot, and she pushed off his scarred moccasin and set the foot firmly on the leather. With swift ease, she traced the outline with charcoal from the fire, pushed the foot aside, and sliced out the strange shape of a Cheyenne moccasin.

Cleve found that watching her dissipated his attention to the cries of his son enough so they didn't trouble him quite so much. He obediently changed feet and watched her cut out the other moccasin.

Then she handed him the leather and several thongs and gestured for him to punch holes and lace the shoes together while she created her own.

"Hey! Listen!" He cocked his head, straining to hear. There was no sound but the soft sighing of the snow-laden wind around the smokehole. "Something's got him!"

She reached to lay her callused hand over his lips. "Yellow Hair, Cheyenne men do not make such a fuss over their young. Indeed, it is the part of their mother's brother to teach them and tease them and watch over them. My own brother, Singing Wolf, should rightfully be the one to do that, but as it is we are too far, and our situation is . . . strange." She smiled mischievously, and he laughed.

"That's right. If you want to get technical, *I'm* his mother, because you are a warrior, and my brothers are way back in Missouri. But is he all right?"

"Of course." She looped a thong expertly through the

holes she had punched in her first moccasin and gathered the leather into the correct shape, arranging the laps to fold around the ankle. "No one came, he got no attention, and so he stopped. Why cry when it gains you nothing and wears you out?"

Cleve thought about that as he painstakingly formed his own footgear. Once you considered it, the system made sense. Children yelled to get what they wanted. If they got nothing by it, they'd stop. He wondered why his own kind hadn't come up with such a simple solution.

Second Son had raced through the construction of her moccasins before the fire needed new fuel, and now she rose to her feet. "Because he has stopped, he will return to his family as a reward," she said.

There was a strained look around her eyes, and Cleve realized that she had been as anxious as he while their child was alone in the thicket. He reached to give her a hug around the hips.

"You're not fooling me," he said. "You want to run out and get him back as much as I do. So go. I'll work on my moccasins while you get him."

She was gone in a rush of displaced air, leaving him smiling down at his work. Almost before he missed her, she returned, her face flushed from the chill, the child clasped tightly to her chest.

Now, standing in the wind, listening for further sounds from the thicket, he remembered his vast relief when he saw that Billy-Wolf had survived his first disciplinary exile.

This was the third. Second Son told him that probably after this the child would remember that his wails earned him nothing but loneliness. Cleve devoutly hoped so, for these times wore on his nerves.

A rushing, hissing crash echoed across the narrow valley. A mass of snow had slipped, he knew, burying the young pines and firs below the western cliffs under yards of chill white.

Until the compacted overhangs had fallen, it would not be safe to try hauling their furs up the sheer walls to the east. The horses would be unable to negotiate the perilous climb Cleve had managed to chip into the rock to allow them to get out of this valley into which they had come with such difficulty.

Snip gave a shiver against his leg and looked toward the thicket again, his ears flicked forward, his tail still. He disapproved of Second Son's baby-training methods even more than his master did, for he adored young Bill. Now he stiffened and growled deep in his throat before shooting toward the fir trees like a black-and-white arrow.

The wolf slipped through a clump of small fir trees, his nose picking up the scent of tender young flesh. It was at some distance from the smoke, but if it had been nearby he would not have hesitated. He must have food. His strength was fading, and if he sank into the snow of the valley's floor he would, he knew, never rise from it again.

There was a lump hanging from a stub of a branch some distance up a tree. An easy leap when he was young and filled with red meat but a hard one now. The wolf gauged the height, gathered his energies, and sprang as high as he could.

His teeth ripped through fur, and the infant screamed with fear. Before the timber wolf could leap again, something black and white shot through the needled branches of the young growth and bowled him over in a drift. Sharp teeth dug into his neck, and he felt his strength oozing away with the blood seeping from those wounds.

Steps crunched in the snow. The dying wolf looked up and saw a big shape, tall against the trees. Then something stabbed into his heart, and he died, his belly still empty, his hunger unsatisfied.

Cleve drew his knife from the skinny creature's heart and pulled Snip away from the ragged, strong-smelling body. He turned to the tree and felt over the bundle that was his son, who was still whimpering softly. He did not scream again, which told his father that the baby had learned his lesson about crying.

He patted the soft cheek and said, "You're all right, little one. You're all right," before turning to pull Snip from the strong-smelling body of the wolf.

He felt Snip over, but except for a slash on the top of his head the dog was unhurt, though his heart was racing beneath his master's hands and his neck hair still bristled. Once Cleve set him down, he moved over beneath the still hanging infant and looked up, whining softly.

A step sounded behind Cleve, and he turned to see Second Son coming through the thicket, headed toward the tree where the baby was hung. She stopped when she saw the dead wolf, and her face went very still. She said nothing, however, as she moved lithely past her husband and checked on their son.

She took the child from the tree and hung the thong around her shoulders. Billy-Wolf hiccupped quietly but made no sound, and Cleve felt with gratitude that he was going to be all right now. No more exile into the tree! Now he would be safely in the tipi, where he belonged.

Thinking about the long journey through country where hostile people roamed, to the fork Terrebonne had spoken of, down on the Green River, Cleve knew that it would be far safer for them all because his son had been taught the Cheyenne way. Wild rivers and rough mountains lay between their home and the rendezvous.

Wilder people, both red and white, inhabited those reaches, and by now Cleve was hardened to the knowledge that they would kill him or Second Son or the infant as quickly as they would anything else, game or man. Life was cheap, here in the Shining Mountains.

Another slithering crash resounded through the cold air. Let the fresh snow fall as it would, the earth was warming, and the foundations of the thick layers above were softening with spring. In a few weeks now he and his family would climb out and begin the long trek down from the Absarokas that would lead across the backbone of these mountains and down into the lower country along the Green.

He turned, sighing, into the tipi, where the coals glowed red and Second Son waited, nursing their son and watching meat roast over the fire. This was a lazy, contented life, once the trapping was done, but he was more than ready for a change.

The smell of the air made him restless, and a feeling of anticipation rippled through his nerves. Soon they would go. He was more than ready.

His old teacher among those in the Ashworth group had told him about occasional random meetings among trappers. There was drinking, carousing, fighting . . .

Cleve felt his heart beat faster at the thought of trying his strength against that of others who were tough enough to live here in the mountains.

He'd tried to drink once, when one of the neighbors brought Pa a jug of applejack. He hadn't had time to drink anything but a sip, which tasted awful, but he still remembered the beating Pa had given him for stealing his liquor. He had a hankering to try again, this time with nobody to punish him for it.

He glanced over at Second Son. As if reading his thoughts, she smiled, her dark eyes sparkling in the red light of the fire. He wondered what she would make of the goings-on when numbers of whites got together.

Cleve yawned and stretched. Being a man, he was finding, was a lot better than being somebody's boy. He was ready to meet other men and trade blows and furs and lies. The sooner the better.

Billy-Wolf gave a quiet gurgle, and Snip jerked and twitched in his sleep. Until then, Cleve thought, stretching, this was the best of lives.

chapter
— 2 —

Lifelong habit pulled at Second Son, making her long to change her campsite when the weather warmed, the snow melted, and small birds began singing their spring songs. Now their deep valley, a shelter when the blizzards blew, became a trap, its walls seeming to lean inward, ready to fall on her as she did the things necessary before they could take the trail out.

Shadow, her mare, felt the compulsion of the season's change as well. She had grown heavy with foal again in the long months since leaving Singing Wolf's village, and now she was very near to her time.

Second Son watched her carefully, for they could not risk her on the terrible climb out of the valley until she delivered her colt. The footing was precarious and the ramp Cleve had chipped was narrow. Her distended belly would make her too wide for the trail.

The young stallion that Second Son had stolen from the Pawnee in years past could make it without trouble, as could Socks, Cleve's gelding, and the horses they had taken from Henri Lavallette's winter camp. But the heavy mare was stuck until her load lightened.

Second Son's own offspring was growing by the day. Young Billy-Wolf was not fat, yet he was becoming longer, stronger, and more alert, his dark eyes snapping toward every sound, his hands reaching, his feet kicking as if trying to walk. He objected to his cradleboard more than any child she had seen; she could only suppose it was his father's blood that made him so impatient with confinement.

Yet he had learned his lesson well. He made no sound, except when she set him on her knee and talked to him, both in the English she had learned from Cleve and Holy William and in her own tongue, which she was determined that he would understand.

When he met her brother Singing Wolf, she wanted him to be able to talk with his uncle. The two of them were destined to be companions, she felt, for Wolf Sings on the Mountain was a kindred name and totem to that of Singing Wolf.

She was carrying her son on her back, tied firmly into his board, when she went to check on Shadow. It was now spring, even in the high country, and the streams ran loudly with snowmelt, the green plants were already knee high, and the overhangs of snowpack had fallen and disappeared among the rocks lining the cliffs.

The mare was standing, head down, in her favorite patch of grass. Her gaze was thoughtful when it met that of Second Son, and when she put out her nose and snuffled at her warrior's hand it was absent-mindedly, as if she listened to something inside herself.

Second Son recognized the signs, for it had not been long since she had done the same, waiting for her son to come to birth. That had been a day etched in her memory, for it also brought an end to her old enemy Jules Terrebonne. The thought of leaving him bound to a tree, waiting for the cold or a grizzly to make an end to him, was a deep satisfaction to her.

She stroked the mare's ears, scratched under her chin, and clucked softly. An inquiring gurgle from behind made her smile and turn so the child could also look into the horse's eyes.

Already the boy was fascinated by their animals, and it

proved that his Cheyenne heritage was strong. Her people were natural horsemen, and he showed signs of following in their ways. That was a necessity in the world of the plains and mountains, and she felt certain that he would surpass his father in riding skills.

Cleve, whatever his other virtues, did not become a part of Socks when he rode, though the horse was trained to do things that it never would have occurred to any of her kind to teach a mount.

The mare gave a long sigh, followed by a groan of effort. The warrior woman laid her hand on her neck and closed her eyes. Shadow was growing old, and Second Son had noticed all her life that older animals tended to have more difficulty with birth. This would not be the first time her mare had trouble at this point.

But it was early yet. The colt was a long way from being born. She turned at last and went to the tipi, where she found Cleve cleaning mud off his outer moccasins and cursing softly, as Snip warmed himself by the fire.

"Yellow Hair, why do you sing that song?" she asked. She hung the cradleboard from its post, which was fixed into the ground, and turned her attention to the venison hanging above the blaze on a tall tripod.

After giving the meat a twirl, which scattered droplets of fragrant steam into the coals, she began rolling the furs that had made their bed for so long. It was getting to be too warm for buffalo robes and beaver blankets.

"This damn mud is sticky as glue. I don't know how we're going to move once we get out of here, if we ever do. The horses may mire up to their bellies, if the top of the ridge is like the bottom of the valley."

That was the sort of silly statement she had learned was peculiar to white men. "The ridge is drained well, for the water came down here. When we get up there the ground will be covered with damp fir and spruce needles, anyway.

"Why do you fret? We will go when we can go and not before. Be patient and play with your son, if you have nothing better to do."

This was a sharper statement than she usually offered, no matter how irritable he became, and he glanced up, concerned. "Shadow?" he asked, knowing that some private worry would explain the tartness of her tone.

She nodded as she tied the thongs holding their blankets rolled together. "She is getting old, Yellow Hair. She has been my friend since I had only twelve seasons, and if she should die it would make me sad. She seems all right, but I have seen old mares die, unable to push the colt out."

"There are things to do for that," he said. "Don't you remember how I helped her when I was a guest of the Burning Hearts?"

Second Son suddenly recalled that long-ago scene, almost forgotten in the difficulties and dangers of their lives since that time. He had, indeed, saved her mount by reaching in and easing the colt through without breaking its legs or its neck. White men, for all their strange ways, had skills that were valuable.

"I forgot." She smiled. "That makes me feel much happier. Will you go with me to see how she is doing?"

"The venison is almost ready. I have a space in my belly that you could put that mare into. After we eat, I'll see what can be done." He wiped his hands on his buckskin breeches and reached for the meat knife.

They left Snip to watch the baby when they returned to the grass patch to check on Shadow. If this was like the situation they had faced before, it would take both to bring the colt. Second Son dreaded that, but as they neared the mare's retreat they heard a soft whicker, followed by a thin bleat of sound.

She had done it alone! Cleve reached for Second Son's hand and they ran together to see the newcomer.

Still dark with wet, the little creature turned to face them, its head down, its sides heaving. Then it reversed itself and began nuzzling beneath the mare, looking for her teat. Shadow gazed smugly at them over the spindly-legged foal, and her sigh was one of great relief and satisfaction.

Second Son reached to touch her nose, not getting too near. Then she turned to Cleve. "In three days we can go. She will gain strength now, and we already have the furs ready to haul up the cliff. You can take the horses up one by one and have them ready when we get the last of the bales on the ridge.

"I have become restless here. It is good to move,

Yellow Hair. I cannot think how your people bear to live in houses rooted to the land."

"What are you going to call the little 'un?" he asked her. He was stroking the damp curls of hair along the colt's back, feeling the bony structure of his ribs and spine and the shape of his barrel, as well as the conformation of his legs.

She walked around to look at the head, which emerged between its mother's legs from time to time as it butted too hard and lost the teat. A jagged streak of white marked the face from nose to forelock.

"Blaze will do well," she said. "And he will belong to our son. Bill and Blaze—in English those go together well, do they not?"

He grinned at her, and she felt once again the surge of warmth that this pale-eyed husband of hers so often gave her. He was not like the Tsistsistas in many ways. He had a gentleness that the men of her tribe seldom allowed to show. But he had a sense of humor that they appreciated a great deal. It was no mistake when she captured him for her "wife," back on the Belle Fourche.

It took three days of constant effort to take the bales of plews up the cliff from their high cave. Cleve climbed to the top, taking the animals up one by one and securing them on a picket line. Then he let down the rawhide ropes.

Second Son, who had the surest of feet, clambered about the cavern high in the cliff, which had sheltered their furs from the damp of winter. She tied the line around each bale, pushing it over the lip of the cave to swing free, and then leaned out perilously to give it a boost upward.

Cleve harnessed Socks's strength in raising the heavy bales. They had spent days making the strong rawhide lines, and a pair of them was passed around a smoothed log forming a pulley. Socks moved on command, walking away and drawing the line smoothly over the wooden roller, until he reached a point at which Cleve could reach the bale and swing it onto the clifftop, once it cleared the edge.

Used to farm work back in Missouri, the gelding didn't object to his task, though the other horses protested when Cleve tried them at it. Every day saw more of the bales in place, protected from the weather by dressed deer hides and the batwing shape of buffalo hide that had formed the walls of their tipi.

Snip prowled below, staring up at his master and Second Son, whimpering softly from time to time and keeping an eye on Bill, who was, as usual, hung high in a tree, faced so he could see his parents at work. Second Son knew that no danger could approach the child without the dog's giving warning, so she worked, unworried, until all the plews were secured.

Now it was time to leave this hidden valley. She had seen it first when she was very young, newly admitted as a warrior to the band. Her brother had stood up there on that cliff, pointing downward and saying that this was a good place to remember.

"If you are ever pursued by enemies too numerous to fight alone, remember this place. It may serve you well as a refuge." The words were addressed to Red Fox, who was the leader of their group of youngsters, but she had never forgotten, and so it had proved.

Those enemies who had followed them the summer before had not ventured past the valley filled with smoke and bubbling mud. Or if they had, they had never thought to look into this forbidding place into which they would have to let themselves and their horses down with rawhide lines. From above it seemed uninhabited, she knew, for they made certain of that after setting up their tipi.

Still, it had been a place that had seen much happiness and some sadness. She thought of their friend Holy William, now lying alone in the valley to the west, his grave guarded by the bones of Jules Terrebonne, which were probably scattered now by scavengers.

Holy William had been a friend, however much she had distrusted him at first. She felt saddened that he never saw his small namesake, for he had anticipated the child's birth with pleasure. Used to the terrible mortality that could overtake the very young, she had never seen a man who seemed so intensely interested in the arrival of a child.

But her people did not brood over death, no matter if the lost one was young or old, for that distracted the mind and wasted energy. She turned again to descend into the valley and take her son down from the branch where he was hung. Snip wagged frantically around her legs as she signalled to Cleve, atop the cliff, that she was ready to begin that last climb. He dropped the rope to her, and she looped it about her and the cradleboard.

The rock was slick with wet as she set her moccasins carefully, balancing the cradleboard on her back as Cleve kept tension on the line from above.

Billy-Wolf was quiet as they went up the face of the rock, using the old ascent rather than the one hacked out for the horses. She felt able to climb all day—to fly like the hawk already poised on a column of air, waiting for prey to appear below. His scream echoed between the walls of the valley as she went up and gained the top.

They were going to travel through the mountains, to visit a place where she would meet others like Yellow Hair. Although she had been taught from birth to suppress her emotions, she felt a flutter of excitement deep inside.

There were weapons, Cleve told her, even finer than those they had from Lavallette's store. There were metal implements as useful as cookpots and knives, for which they could trade plews. Again the excitement welled up in her, but she suppressed it sternly and stepped out onto the top of the cliff.

Cleve waited, and together they loaded the bales onto the restless horses, who were snuffling and whinnying with this unexpected change in their routine. Then they turned their mounts to follow this ridge to the obscure path by which they had come.

They were alert; Snip ranged ahead, his nose in the air, sniffing for danger. This was their world, and it contained, Second Son knew all too well, a multitude of enemies.